Michael Linford

As the Wolf Howls

To Victoria,
Thank you for your
support !

love Michael

First published 2016
by Rowanvale Books Ltd
Imperial House
Trade Street Lane
Cardiff
CF10 5DT
www.rowanvalebooks.com

A CIP catalogue record for this book is available from the British
Library.
ISBN: 978-1-910832-23-3

'To look into the eyes of a wolf is to see your soul. Just be sure something you want to view is there.'

- Unknown

This book is dedicated to all those whose lands have become lost, and to my little tribe for their love and constant support.

PROLOGUE

The flames leapt higher, engulfing the settlement almost instantly. Through the thick smoke Majila could see them searching and destroying everything in their path. The screams emanating from his burning village tore at his heart. It was as if he felt every bit of pain being inflicted on his tribe; he did not feel any physical pain though, it was more than that, far more. Each deathly scream stripped away another layer of his inner being and he was almost rooted to the spot where he crouched, hidden from those responsible for all this death and destruction.

He watched as familiar faces were dragged out into the clearing by their hair; he watched their fear and agony as they bravely fought the attackers as best they could. His people were not fighters by nature, and although they struggled bravely to defend themselves, it was all in vain. Before his eyes, all manner of violence became them. As the smoke rose higher he was able to see more clearly the land where his village had stood just hours before. The huts that hadn't already burned to the ground were engulfed in flame and heading towards the same fate.

In the open land before him he saw bodies, dozens of them, lying bloodied and lifeless in piles scattered everywhere. His pain intensified as he saw not just elders, but women and children too. All killed by this force that he had not seen before and knew nothing about. The men moved in a group past the newly slaughtered settlers and on further into the burning village. At once, he leapt to his feet and ran out into the smoke. Quickly stepping in a half-crouched position, he made his way to the last of the elders he had watched them kill. He bent down and gently turned the lifeless elder's head towards him; the blood covered his hands as he knelt by the limp body and whispered words, seemingly to himself: 'Take these souls lightly, dear Mother, and let the light of the moon grant them a chance again, with nothing but goodness in their hearts. Let them begin a new journey.' He closed his eyes and stayed quiet for a long moment, deep in thought, trying to send each and every lost soul into the safety of the spirit world's embrace.

As he opened his eyes, his blood ran cold. In all the

confusion he had forgotten about Aalym and their child. Aalym was supposed to have gone out into the woods, taking Esmee with her, so she could start to learn about the forest, its spirits and the power it wields. But that morning Esmee had been restless and Aalym decided it wasn't the right time for her first lessons. They must have been here when the attacks started! The realisation made Majila leap to his feet and run directly through the flames, towards their hut. The heat hit him before he got close enough to see that his hut was raging with flames that shot up high into the sky and lapped at the trees behind them. Majila thundered through the flames, bursting into the hut, before throwing himself to the coolest part, the clay floor. He crawled through, calling for Aalym, struggling to make his way through the heat and thick smoke that threatened to push him back further. In the distance, he heard a cry and within seconds he made it through the fire to their eating quarters. The place was destroyed; tribal artefacts lay smashed everywhere and in the corner, crouched behind an upturned table, were Aalym and Esmee. He raced towards them and threw his arms around them both. Esmee was hysterical as she wrapped her arms around his neck, howling into his chest.

'It's all going to be okay, Esmee, I'll get us out of here and we'll be safe.' As he said the words, he felt a warm sensation running down his arm and pooling at his elbow. Esmee noticed too and wailed even harder than before, turning her face deeper into him and letting his body envelope her completely. 'Aalym, my love, we have to move. We need to run for safety. We can make it if we go now.' It took Aalym's lack of response before Majila realised that it was *her* blood running over him, not his. Hidden beneath her bowed head was a ragged stone, shaped like an arrowhead and stuck deep into her throat. The blood was seeping out from around the stone and was flowing at a constant rate.

'Majila, my warrior, you cannot save me now. Take Esmee and get away to safety, it is your only hope. These men came for you and the one your magic also dwells in. It is not safe for you two here; with my blessing to guide you, you must leave now.' The words were whispered, her pain overwhelming as she spoke each one.

'I cannot leave you. You are my Aalym, my heart, my lifeblood, I won't leave you,' he said, shaking as he cradled her and pleaded for her to hold on.

'You must, my love. There is no time and you must save Esmee. All our fates are in your hands now and we need you more than ever. It is your time to be the leader that destiny has always foreseen for you. Please go, I beg you, save our child and know that I am always with you.'

Majila choked back tears as he held her closer and, in that instant, he knew she was right. Her life was slipping away in his arms; he could feel her breath slowing and saw as her eyes struggled to cling onto their last view of this world. He leant forward and kissed her, releasing all his pain and hers in one last act of passion. 'I love you, Aalym, and I always will. My heart waited for you and will wait forever to be with yours again. Travel without fear and let my love light the way for you, as yours will mine, eternally.' He felt the last of her breath leave her and gently lowered her to the floor. Once more, he leant down, kissing her soft mouth, and then with his finger he wiped one of his tears and traced a soft line down her forehead. He removed a necklace and placed it gently around her neck, his last token of a love that blinded him and gave him complete awareness in equal measures.

He wiped away his tears and struggled to his feet. His legs felt weak and his heart felt more lost than ever before. Esmee was looking up at him with a mixture of confusion and sadness and he knew that one day she would understand just how strong the bond of their family's love had been. The fire was beginning to threaten the room they were in now and Majila knew that he had to move quickly to stand any chance of getting himself and Esmee to freedom. He grabbed a long animal-skin cloak and threw it around himself, gathering some things that they'd need on their journey. They didn't have long before any escape would be completely cut off by the fire. He threw some food and things that would be of use into a cloth sack and quickly tried to plot their best chance of escape.

He felt a small hand tugging at his cloak and looked down to see Esmee, wrapped up in her own cloak, holding out the harness that Majila had made for her when she began to walk. It had been a surprise for Aalym and it meant that she could still go for the walks at sunset she so loved, but with Esmee safely strapped to her back. He'd made it out of skins and fur; it had taken a long time to make it sturdy enough that it was safe, but once completed, it had been a great help to Aalym, and Esmee loved being up so high that she could see everything but still feel so protected. Majila's daydreaming was cut short by the sound of their wooden hut crackling louder as the fire grew. He took the sling and lifted Esmee onto his back. She was wrapped up tightly and wriggled into her comfortable position, with her tiny hands placed firmly on her father's broad shoulders. 'You are a clever girl, Esmee. I promise you that we will be okay. We must go now, so stay quiet and we will find safety.'

Majila took her right hand in his and placed a small string of his beads in it. Then, with the fire's strength gaining, he threw a blanket over both of them and headed back the way he had entered. The fire had risen, which left the roof's strength dangerously unpredictable, but it meant the floor was barely smouldering now and perfect for escape. Majila crouched and, with Esmee on his back, scuttled through the main area, and out into the night. Once outside he threw the smoking blanket back into the hut, desperate to leave no signs of an escape if the men came back for a second search, and listened for any sounds of these same men who had destroyed his village. The only sounds he could hear came from the centre of the village and, without looking, he knew that the last of the bodies were being piled up in the clearing, ready to be disposed of. *These men came for you and the one your magic also dwells in.* Aalym's words haunted him as he pictured the suffering of his people. They had missed his daughter though and now the two of them needed to find safety before the men came looking further.

Majila stood straight, the dark night and the smoke acting as a perfect cover for their escape. Quickly but carefully, he stepped into the woods and, with his beautiful daughter on his back, journeyed into the unknown.

CHAPTER 1

Black Wolf woke with a start and sat upright in his bedding, his body dripping with sweat. It was the third night in a row that he had had that same dream. He sat there gathering his thoughts whilst his breathing returned to normal. Every time he woke up it was the same; he was frozen in some strange kind of fright and his body was soaked. All he remembered was the fire, seen through the eyes in his dream — fire reaching towards the sky, devouring everything it touched. He knew in the dream he was running, but did not know why or where. He lay back down but couldn't escape the strange feeling that smothered him. He was a warrior. He had faced great dangers in battle and hunted the most vicious of animals, yet now he was haunted by his own rest. Sleep was not returning to him this night, he was sure, so he pulled on his cloak and headed out of his hut.

The first lights of morning cast a blue tinge to the sky and there were just a few fading reminders of any stars that illuminated the campsite the previous night. As he looked around the camp, he noticed a figure sat by the fire that was dwindling in the morning dew. He stood, quietly stretching, and made his way over to the figure. As he got closer he realised it was Grey Moon, the eldest of the tribe and certainly the wisest. He had been with them seemingly since time began and although he wasn't in charge, any decisions that were made always included him. Everyone regarded him as a sage; the others knew he harnessed great powers but never pushed him on the subject, sometimes out of fear but mainly out of respect.

'Come sit, Black Wolf. There's nothing to fear from the fire, I promise. Join me for a while and we can talk comfortably.'

Black Wolf hadn't even got close to Grey Moon but, as always, there wasn't a chance of anyone doing anything without Grey Moon knowing.

'Couldn't sleep, Wolf? Or am I such good company that you chose to leave your night world to join me?'

Black Wolf sensed a slight flicker of amusement on the old man's face and wondered just how much he knew.

'Your company is always a privilege, Grey Moon, I

agree, but I'm up this morning as I was disturbed in my night world.'

Black Wolf sat on the mat opposite Grey Moon, across from the fire, and stared at the dying embers before him.

'The fire again, my child?'

Black Wolf sat open-mouthed, but before he could reply, Grey Moon spoke again.

'There is a time in all our lives where we must learn something. Our people have learned most through their journeys into the night world, but sadly this is a custom that few respect anymore. It appears the gods speak to you, Black Wolf, and want you to follow this path. Yours is the strongest voice of the young... Maybe you need to listen and go to the places where all truths are told?'

Grey Moon always spoke in seemingly deep, prophetic riddles, but there was always something about him that could never be ignored.

'I have listened to your stories of the night world journeys many times, Grey Moon. I have never had a vision like that though, just this dream which wakes me. It has no question or answer, there is just the fire and then I wake!'

Grey Moon laughed softly to himself; his whole body shook and his face creased with a mixture of pleasure and frustration. 'Trust me, Black Wolf, this is a journey. I think you should follow it and then you will find all the answers you seek. I have much faith in you and I have a gift to give you which I hope will aid you on your way.'

From his lap, Grey Moon handed a small package to Black Wolf. It was a small wooden box with delicate engravings on it. There were five carvings in total: a rock, a stream, a flame and a small, billowing cloud. The fifth carving was an eye and was placed in the centre, with the other four placed at each corner. Black Wolf opened the box and inside was a small leather-bound book. All the pages of the book were blank and there was a precious little metal clasp on the front. It was an exquisite gift but Black Wolf had no idea why he deserved it, or where it had come from.

'Why, Grey Moon? It's beautiful, but why me? And where did it come from?'

Grey Moon poked around in the ashes of the fire and answered slowly. 'The box has been in my possession for years, waiting for a purpose, and the book gives it that purpose. The book is a journal for you and I got it as payment for some help I gave within the walls of the great city. All I ask is that you write in it your thoughts, your feelings and your dreams, for the journeys into the night world are the most important.'

When he finished, Grey Moon stood slowly and wrapped himself up in his cloak.

'I don't know what to say, Grey Moon. I will do all you ask and I hope this will make sense of my dreams, for it's true that I am haunted by this fire and long to discover what this all means.'

Black Wolf also stood and took the old man's hands in his before embracing him.

'I must rest now, Black Wolf. Thank you for your company and good luck with your quest. With enough patience, you will find your path reveals itself to you with great ease.' Grey Moon smiled once more and started to walk back to his own hut.

Black Wolf sat back down by the fire, turning the book over in his hands. It was a beautiful creation and he found himself excited at the thought of using it. 'Thank you,' he called after the elder. 'I will cherish it and I look forward to showing you when I have done some work within its beautiful pages. Sleep well, Grey Moon.'

The old man heard him call out and waved to respond as he pulled open the covers of his hut. 'Good luck, child. I wish I could see your work too. The fire holds no fear but sadly the spark that causes it does.'

The words Grey Moon spoke were too low for Black Wolf to hear, and with tired bones and a heavy heart, Grey Moon settled down to sleep.

Black Wolf lay down by the last of the fire and stared up at the sky, his thoughts no longer consumed by his dream of fire but of Grey Moon instead. He seemed so old now and Black Wolf often thought how sad it was that he was so alone, even in the camp. Black Wolf knew that the others found it hard to spend time with Grey Moon. They never knew what to talk about with him, as his own story was a closely guarded secret that seemingly only he himself knew. He had no children but Black Wolf knew what that kind of loss was like as he'd lost his own parents when he was just a baby. Grey Moon had always been there for him and they had formed a friendship over the years, so it wasn't a surprise that he'd given Black Wolf lessons on how to discover even more of the world around him.

Black Wolf often thought of Grey Moon as having some sort of burden which maybe one day he would share, but in all the time they had spent together this had never happened, and he knew better than to try to force anything out of him.

As he lay there, Black Wolf studied the box again. He couldn't understand the significance behind the carvings, but they were beautiful and he knew he would cherish both the box and the book forever. Inserting the book carefully back inside the box, he placed it next to him and closed his eyes. The fire was gone, but the burning embers created a nice enough heat for him to relax.

Had he opened his eyes at that moment, he would've noticed that the symbol of a rock on the lid of the box was glowing bright red. Unaware of this strange event, Black Wolf sighed deeply and drifted off to sleep.

CHAPTER 2

When Black Wolf awoke after a few hours, he found it was a lot later in the morning than he thought. The campsite was a hive of activity, and many of the tribe were out of their huts doing a variety of chores. It always amazed him just how busy the tribe could keep themselves and he often sat and watched them going about their work. The children were playing in large groups in front of the biggest hut. This hut had been made as a place for them to learn, but any lessons usually started in the early afternoon when the children had run themselves out of excess energy and were ready to sit calmly and be taught. Grey Moon had been one of the main reasons that the school had been built but he had never taught there. Black Wolf had asked him once if he'd ever thought of teaching there and he had told of his own personal dislike for teaching within what he believed to be very strict structures.

The more Black Wolf thought about Grey Moon, the more he realised what a truly great man he was. A man who had more answers than questions but also one that easily assumed a role of someone with nothing to offer compared to others. He was a truly complex individual but one of Black Wolf's favourite people to spend time with. With this thought in his mind, he stood up and looked for him. Apart from the children running wild, there were many more things going on around him. This native land was alive with both work and play today. There were the eldest of the tribe, sat together, talking or fixing clothing. The females of the tribe were busy cleaning and cooking, while the men were fixing the huts and making plans for other work that needed doing. There was only one thing that Black Wolf wanted to do though, and that was to find Grey Moon so he could talk to him some more about his journal, the night world and where he was heading with all of this. He saw no sign of him as he searched the campsite, so he headed for his hut to see if he was still asleep. Passing through the various groups of people he felt a twinge of regret; most of the tribe had family and that's what made their population so big, but Black Wolf was on his own. People spoke to him regularly and seemed to think of him quite highly, given what he had provided the tribe since arriving, but it didn't alter the fact that he was alone. He wondered if that was what had created such a bond with Grey Moon, for despite their difference in age, ideas or beliefs they were both solitary, and as a result had pulled together and always been there for each other.

Black Wolf arrived at Grey Moon's hut and found it open; he knocked on the hard frame of the doorway and entered. There was no sign of life in the hut and Black Wolf never felt comfortable in someone else's home unless they were there, so he set out again. He pulled the cover over the door and walked back across the site. For the first time since he'd woken up, Black Wolf looked at the sky. It was a beautiful clear day and already getting warm. He was thankful for the cooling breeze that was blowing across and keeping the barren floor from baking underneath his feet. He made it to his hut and was just about to go inside and lock himself away when he noticed a note, half hidden under the door cover. It was a note from Grey Moon.

'I didn't want to wake you. I headed out early, towards the river, and will be there until late afternoon. If you wish to join me, your company would be most welcome. If you are too busy then I will come and find you later. Speak soon, Grey Moon.'

Black Wolf laughed to himself at the thought of being too busy. Grey Moon knew he had nothing to do, unless he chose to, but they still wouldn't assume anything about each other. This respectful thinking was one of many ways that their friendship worked so successfully. Black Wolf had no particular wish to go too far today, but in his heart he longed to be around Grey Moon, wherever he was. He threw some food and other things into a sack, slung it over his shoulder and headed off to find his wise old friend.

The river was a long walk out of the campsite but Black Wolf couldn't think of many more beautiful places to spend a day. The whole campsite was circled by a ring of woodland, enough trees to be of use to the tribe for hunting or timber, but not enough that they were of any trouble, and they never stopped the tribe making trips around their land. Black Wolf felt calmer when he reached the woods; it was a welcome pleasure for him just to have the peace and quiet. The only sounds around him were the animals around the trees and the crunching of twigs under his feet.

This is where Black Wolf had been discovered as a child, wrapped in fur and left in a hollowed-out tree stump. Someone had found him and brought him back to the tribe. The women at the camp had almost fought each other to look after him; they had all said how they felt drawn to him but couldn't explain why. They put it down to the sadness of such a beautiful child being unloved and abandoned. Even in his childhood he was powerful to look at. A combination of his strong features, slightly tanned skin and deep hazel eyes made him look far from helpless and abandoned. It always amazed Black Wolf how much he loved this place. He realised though that this was because he had been here at such a young age and had been so well looked after before being discovered, the place held only good memories for him. The forest had taken the place of a mother to him. Today wasn't a day to spend time here though; he was eager to find Grey Moon and enjoy a day in his old friend's company.

Coming out of the woods, he saw his friend straight away — sat in front of the river, seemingly glowing under the baking sun.

'I'm so glad you could join me, my young friend. I hope my disappearance didn't cause you worry?'

Black Wolf walked over to Grey Moon and sat down next to him.

'I was curious as to where you had gone, Grey Moon, but I know you are more than capable of looking after yourself. You know how different I feel from the others and how much I long for solitude, but with you it's different; you are like a father to me and I enjoy spending time sitting with you and talking.'

Black Wolf noticed as Grey Moon shifted slightly, uncomfortably, and briefly closed his eyes, seemingly lost in some painful thought, before relaxing again and speaking.

'My child, you are more like family to me than anyone and it fills my heart with joy to hear you speak so highly of me. Times are changing for all of us — especially for you and me — and it's important for us to talk away from the tribe. We are different and that is why we get treated in such a way. In your life, things have already changed. You remember going into battles with other tribes, hunting and providing for the people, but now we have a settled peace.

Do you not wonder why all our people seem so busy all the time, but you and I have nothing to do? We get fed and are free to roam when we please, without a question asked — why is that?'

Black Wolf had been thinking the same for quite some time now but never asked anyone, always nervous of what the answer might be.

'I always thought I wasn't meant to be involved, being an outsider. Apart from my strength, which was useful in battles and hunting, I have nothing to offer the tribe and they know that. You are our eldest father and I imagined that gave you every right to roam as freely as you wish.'

Grey Moon laughed; it was a deep, hearty sound that rumbled up through his chest and shook him. He placed his hand on Black Wolf's shoulder and looked him directly in the eyes. 'My boy, you have more to offer the tribe than you could ever imagine and they know that, which is why you have no rules to follow. We have elders who guide us, but no leader. He is waiting for the elements to provide him with the vision he needs. His destiny is starting to reveal itself now!'

'Who is this leader though, Grey Moon? When will we meet him?' Black Wolf was excited at the thought of the tribe becoming a solid unit under a strong leader.

'It is you, child. Your path is already clearing but you must begin to walk it. The fire was the first sign and you must now look deep within yourself. It is like tracking someone through the snow; their path gets covered by a fresh blanket but, if you look hard enough, their footprints are still there! Find yourself, Wolf, and you will stand at the head of our people with great power.'

Black Wolf could hardly believe what he was hearing; surely he wasn't meant for such greatness? As much as he couldn't believe it though, he knew Grey Moon was a prophet and all he said held strength amongst his people. Black Wolf thought about the fire and shuddered. Could he walk through those flames and find the answers?

'I need to know more, Grey Moon. Can you help me find the truth? We have all day to work on this.'

Grey Moon smiled brightly. 'We will, Wolf, but be patient. First we have something to do today.'

'What is it, Grey Moon? Are we going travelling?'

Grey Moon smiled again and patted a cloth bag by his side. He opened it to reveal long, sharply carved sticks, some thread and hooks.

'First, we fish!' he said, grinning. Black Wolf sat next to him looking confused at first but then started rolling with laughter.

CHAPTER 3

Across the river, high up on a plateau in the mountains, stood Orgent. The tribe referred to it merely as 'the great walled city', and they chose to have no familiarity with the place if they could. To the tribe it was a place shrouded in mystery and, due to the high wall that surrounded it, a place to fear. The only member of the natives ever to enter its large oak doors was Grey Moon. He had been there a few times and though people were desperate to know why he had been, or what he saw inside, they never asked. Grey Moon was the eldest and most respected of the tribe and they knew better than to try to force information from him. If they needed to know, he would tell them. The main reason that the natives feared Orgent was because of the wall and the secrecy that came with it. These were people who lived on open land, free to roam and with no boundaries, so they couldn't understand why someone would choose to lock themselves away. Many tales were told around campfires of a dark magic that lived in Orgent, of strange creatures and the evil that dwelt there. None of these storytellers had seen it for themselves though; they merely passed on fables and added their own twists to make a chilling story. Only Grey Moon knew the truth.

Orgent had a vast population of people who lived happily within its huge walls. In the far north of the city was the temple, a huge white structure that provided a stunning backdrop to the rest of the city. The temple housed the emperor, his daughter and many more people who were staff, such as servants, advisors and a healer. It was a huge building with many floors and even with all the people inside, there was still lots of space left untouched. Around the perimeter of the city were buildings of different sizes and shapes, also white in colour, which were home to the many people who lived there. With the city so high up in the mountains, and full of white buildings, in fables it was referred to as the 'city of clouds', well camouflaged amongst the vast sky when clouds appeared. In the centre of the city was a large, open courtyard, which was used for many purposes throughout the year. Any sacred bindings between couples were performed here, as were all large celebrations. The markets were constructed here every day too, full of food, clothing and crafts that were sold to the city dwellers. The markets were only open for a short time daily, but still they managed to provide anything that was needed. Once the market closed, the stalls were carefully taken down again and stored for the next day's trade.

At night, the whole city was so empty that apart from the few lanterns glowing above the walls, there was nothing to see. Even the night guards were cloaked in the surrounding darkness, invisible to the naked eye, keeping watch while the city slept. The last few nights had been so black though that despite their training and attention to detail, the guards hadn't noticed the shadows hidden near the foot of the walls. The dark figures, almost blacker than the night, moved swiftly but never near the light. While the city carried on with its normal routine, the shadows sat and waited.

CHAPTER 4

Amelia sat and looked out over Orgent; from her sleeping quarters she could see for miles. The people of Orgent often talked about the princess, speculating about how lavish her life must be and what she spent her days doing. In truth, Amelia was dissatisfied with most aspects of her life. She spent most of her time looking out over the huge walls and daydreaming of being on the other side, free to travel and explore the vast wilderness that she had never seen. Her life as the emperor's daughter in this great city left her feeling empty and she didn't know why. She often walked around the city and found herself envying the people with normal lives and freedom. She knew she was blessed to never struggle like most people did but, somewhere deep within her, she wanted to. Her longing for adventure had grown ever since she was a little girl and now, as an adult, she felt more trapped than ever.

Most of her days were spent within the walls of the temple and she felt a sadness that this was her whole life passing before her eyes. One day her father would die and all this would be hers; she wanted none of it though. Amelia wanted to run, escape from the shackles of this stale comfort and throw herself into a world of uncertainty, passion and fate. That was the world where she belonged, even though her father dismissed all talk of it.

Amelia could understand her father's worries. He had vowed never to let her out of his reach after her mother had died. Since that terrible night when he had lost his love, the emperor had kept a tighter watch on Amelia than ever. As she had approached adulthood her cage grew bigger — but she knew it was still a cage. She often thought of her mother and wondered if dying was so bad, compared to a life unlived.

Amelia had only been young when her mother had died; it wasn't until she was older that she'd been told the full story.

One night her mother had got out of the bed she shared with the emperor and walked across the room to the large window. He had been woken by the noise of her opening the large iron locks and called out to her, asking what she was doing, but she didn't react — she had simply stepped out onto the ledge and over, disappearing into the black night. The emperor had screamed and hurried to the window, but when he looked down the lifeless body of his love was spread out on the ground. Her long blonde hair billowed in the wind and slowly turned crimson as the blood pooled beneath her.

Amelia remembered that after her mother's death her father had brought in a healer for the city, who had declared that her mother's death was a result of a sickness which causes the sufferer to fall into a madness from which there is no escape — unless treated before becoming sick. The healer worked tirelessly, producing a herbal mixture which all the city's population had to burn in their houses before they slept. The people were so scared of this sickness that they all followed the emperor's orders without question. Even now, Amelia and all the population were still burning this same herbal cure before they slept. Amelia looked at the ashes in the clay bowl by her bed and wondered just how it could have wiped out such a strong sickness. She didn't mind the smell of the burning herbs at all, it helped her drift off to sleep easily and then, before she knew it, it was morning.

Today, Amelia was determined to head out into the city to look at the markets; she needed to get out into the fresh air. It was early afternoon now, so the markets would be at their busiest and Amelia hoped that the vibrant atmosphere might lift her spirits. She made her way through the hallways and down the staircases of the temple quickly and found her father sitting in the main room. He was sat reading documents and barely looked up as she spoke.

'Father, I am heading to the markets for a short while. I wondered if Elspeth might like to accompany me while I'm out — have you seen her?'

Elspeth was Amelia's maid and her duties were to make sure the princess had everything done for her that was needed. Amelia shunned this idea though and instead they spent time talking and laughing together. They were friends, and Amelia did as much for herself as she could without anyone knowing any different.

'Elspeth just left, dear. She was headed for the markets anyway, so if you go now you should catch her.'

Her father looked deep in thought as he traced the documents with his fingers and seemed keen to carry on without disturbance.

'Thank you, Father. I shall head after her now then. I won't be long!'

With this, Amelia turned and headed for the main door. As she opened it, she glanced back at her father, still buried in his work, and then quietly headed out into the warm air.

CHAPTER 5

Black Wolf's patience had grown thin; Grey Moon stood laughing as Black Wolf muttered angrily to himself. They had been fishing for a few hours but, as usual, Grey Moon had been the only one to catch anything.

'Sometimes it's purely the intention that matters, my child,' he said, and Black Wolf soon found himself laughing too; he knew this time with his friend was not really about fishing anyway and was happy to concede defeat to the wise old hunter.

Once they had all their equipment packed up, they sat on a blanket looking out over the river. On the other side of the bank was a thick forest and behind that the massive mountains of Loyanas. The mountains towered over the tribe's camp and on a clear day you could just see the magnificent snowy peaks reaching high into the sky. The land around their camp was vast, yet Black Wolf had never ventured farther away than within the boundaries of the river.

'I sense you have many questions for me, my friend. I cannot give you all the answers, but I promise to talk as freely as I can. Life is better lived when we still have some unanswered questions; it pushes us to discover those answers for ourselves and we grow in the process.'

Black Wolf's head was spinning with thousands of different questions and he struggled to place them in any order that would help him avoid missing out anything important.

'We have as long as you need, Wolf. Relax and let them ask themselves. We have until nightfall and then you must go search for different answers.' Grey Moon placed his hand on Black Wolf's shoulder and gently encouraged him.

'You spoke earlier of times changing for all of us, especially for you and me — what is this change that you talk of?'

Grey Moon took a deep breath and spoke. 'The mother of us all does her best to care for and nurture us, but she herself can suffer sickness at times and it's usually her children that make her ill. In this world, there are those who have abilities and those who want them. Like gifts, our mother has spread those with abilities around, for too much power can corrupt. They live happily, often not knowing they are special, and every single thing they do makes our mother happy and proud. These other children though, those who want abilities, grow jealous and angry at the others and would be prepared to do anything to get their abilities. This anger bubbles away deep within the heart of these few, making our mother sad and hurt. This bad feeling slowly poisons her until she is helpless to save herself or, indeed, us. That is when she sends her signs through our night sky spirits and asks for help through the night world. Our mother has called to you and needs your help, Black Wolf.'

'I'm just a man though, Grey Moon. What can I do to help? How do you know it's my destiny to be this leader you talk about?'

Grey Moon looked out over the river, his old eyes fixed with determination. 'I see many things, my child. I walk not just through this life but the ones before too. Sometimes a leader misses his chance to right the wrongs because he lacks faith in himself. I have seen this once before and though the evil was stopped, it was never removed for good. I believe that now is the time for the parts to become whole and banish this evil, once and for all. Trust me, you will be the leader. I am ahead of you in this game of fate, yet there is so much I cannot speak of, for you have to discover it for yourself but you will. With your eyes and heart open, you will find your way, trust me.'

Black Wolf listened intently. A part of him felt a surge of familiarity in what his wise friend was telling him, but he still struggled to make sense of the words through all the riddles.

'You said the fire was the start of my journey, Grey Moon. Can you tell me what it means?'

'The night world is a voyage of discovery that we must walk alone, but I can tell you that I too have seen the fire. My view is from the earth and with the sky west, not north. I was suffering, trapped between two worlds, and a young man set me free. He was too late to stop the fire but he saved more than he knew.'

Grey Moon leant forward, his head propped silently in his hands in thought. Black Wolf watched as his friend seemed to battle through all sorts of emotions before returning to a state of calm again.

'Do the tribe know my fate? Do they know who I am? Who am I, Grey Moon?'

Grey Moon was prepared for so many questions from Black Wolf; he expected it and was eager to answer as many as he could. 'The tribe are waiting for a leader to present himself at some point. They don't know who it is but are ready for the sign of proof and will follow that person, whoever it is. You know half of who you are, Wolf. It is up to you to find out the rest. You will during your voyage and then the proof is yours to return to our home and lead your men onwards.'

'What is out there, Grey Moon? What am I preparing to face?'

Grey Moon sighed and once more turned to look Black Wolf in the eyes. 'A great evil, my child, which has travelled through time, for the four pieces of the puzzle needed to become superior. Whether those pieces are kept or destroyed, if they are brought together then evil will win. Our sky will be starless and the night world will no longer exist. Our mother's life is at stake.'

Black Wolf stood up and walked down to the river's edge. This place was so beautiful that you couldn't help but think of nature as being feminine. He himself had thought of the forest as a mother to him, but that was tiny compared to the soul of the earth. That was the mother he was meant to save.

It was late afternoon now and the sun was already slowly falling in the sky. Grey Moon gathered his sack and blanket together while Black Wolf stood staring into the calm waters of the river.

'Let us head back now, Wolf. If you bring the fish, we can eat and then sit by a fire. I feel you have more questions for me and I promise I will try to answer them all.'

Black Wolf folded up the cloth with the fish in it, tied it and threw it over his shoulder. 'I have many more questions, old friend, and I can think of no better way to spend this evening than in your company.'

The two friends set off back through the woods and headed for their camp. They were both silent as they walked together. Grey Moon was enjoying the chance to have time away from the others, while Black Wolf was mulling over all the new information he'd been told. He had a few more questions for Grey Moon but felt that he would have to be alone for a while and work it all out.

When they got back to the camp, it was starting to get dark. They both ate in their own huts and then, after a short time to settle themselves, they met together again. Grey Moon came over to Black Wolf's hut and they were soon sat outside, next to a roaring fire. The nights were starting to get cold and the two old friends sat close to the warmth, ready to continue their conversation. It was Black Wolf who spoke first.

'When you gave me my gift, you said you'd been to the great walled city — what were you doing there?'

'I visit the city often, Wolf. They have a healer who performs a great service to the emperor and he needs herbs. Most of the herbs only grow down here on our land though, so I provide them and get things in return, like your book.'

Black Wolf had many more questions about Orgent but they weren't important compared to all that was happening. Looking at the fire, Black Wolf asked the first thing which came into his head. 'What should I do next?'

Grey Moon threw more wood onto the fire, watching the flames rise and reflect in Black Wolf's eyes. 'You must see the night world's visions and then feel them, for only by feeling them will you truly understand their meaning. Write in the book that I gave you and from the words, more will be revealed to you. You will be leaving here soon and then you will need the skills of the wolf that you are. You will need to track and find, for only when the puzzle is complete can you become what you need to be. Trust me, my friend, more will become apparent to you soon.'

Black Wolf stared into the fire. He could feel something deep inside him, fighting to get out, and for the first time he felt that maybe he did have a destiny to be fulfilled.

'Why was I named Black Wolf? I see the others and they are all given normal names — why are we so different?'

Grey Moon again had that sad look in his eyes, the look of memories that still touched him, years later. 'You were found in the woods by a traveller. He had been trekking across lands for a long time, following a call that leads us to where we are now. When he found you, there was nothing around for a great distance except one sole animal who had seemingly protected you, both day and night. That animal was a large black wolf and when the traveller picked you up to take you to the camp, the wolf bowed his head and simply disappeared into the woods. Our people saw this as a great sign and could think of no better title for you than that of your protector. So you became the Black Wolf.'

Black Wolf felt the tears sting his eyes; he had never known these things. Always longing to know more about his past but never finding the courage to ask — until now. 'What about you, Grey Moon? Can you tell me more of your life?'

Grey Moon poked around in the flames with a stick, watching the sparks fly up and die in the cool night air. 'One day you will learn more about me, my friend. Now is not the time, but you will, I promise. All I ask is that you never judge me when you hear my tale. Anything I do is with the best intentions and not a moment passes where I don't wish that some things could be different. This is our life though, Wolf. What we want isn't always what we get.'

Black Wolf could sense the sadness in his friend and decided not to push him further, he would find out soon enough. 'I would never judge you, Grey Moon, I promise. There's not a soul alive who could judge such a good man as you. I thank you for all your answers today and feel privileged that you are with me on this journey. You are my truest of friends.'

Grey Moon stood slowly and patted Black Wolf on the shoulder. 'I thank you for everything, my friend. You make me happier and prouder than I could ever show you. I'm sorry to leave you, but I must sleep now. It's been a long day and I need my rest; I think now would be a good time for you to lie down too. Let the conversations of today play through your mind and the night world will come calling. Goodnight, dear friend, I will see you in the morning.'

'Goodnight, Grey Moon. Thank you for everything,' Black Wolf replied, and slowly headed into his hut.

The camp was thick with smoke from the dying fires that decorated the ground in various places. Grey Moon entered his hut and settled down for the night, his thoughts on the conversations today and those still to come. At the same time Black Wolf settled down too and, pulling the furs over himself, slowly drifted off to sleep.

CHAPTER 6

The smell of burning was almost gone now and Majila lifted Esmee from his back and set her down by his feet. They had been trekking for over a day now and Majila was desperate to rest. Esmee had slept a lot on the journey, laid against his broad shoulders, as the rhythm of his walking relaxed her. They had trekked through the forest surrounding the burning remains of their camp, and had made it to the snowy mountains beyond. Majila had needed to rest then, the adrenaline already wearing off and leaving him cold and tired, but the fear of capture had pushed him on. They made their way slowly down the mountains, hidden in the falling snow, carefully manoeuvring over large boulders and round the steepest parts of the rock face.

Halfway down, he had found a small cave that provided enough shelter to allow them to rest. He had gathered some branches from the snow-covered trees that dotted the mountain and made a cover, so that once they were in the cave no one would notice. From his sack, he removed a small lamp and lit it, giving them both light and a bit more warmth.

Laying some blankets out, he made a bed for Esmee and motioned for her to lie down. Majila was on his knees and Esmee threw her arms around him and hugged him tightly.

'It's all going to be okay, little one. Tonight we sleep and then tomorrow we walk on again. I will be here by your side all night, don't worry.'

Esmee kissed him on the cheek and lay down, while Majila pulled blankets over her and stroked her golden hair. Before long, she was fast asleep and Majila was sat by the entrance to the cave. The night was cloudy and he knew that there would be more snow falling as they slept. He was glad for the safety of the cave and the warmth it provided; it was all that was keeping them alive and safe this night.

Majila spread out some blankets for himself, next to Esmee, and tried to get some sleep. His thoughts were filled with Aalym. With his eyes shut, he could see her face; her beautiful blue eyes stared straight into his heart, and the pain he felt was so intense it made him ache. The tears rolled down his cheeks until he finally drifted off to sleep.

In the morning, Majila was woken by Esmee and, after eating, they set off again. The mountains were far more perilous today as the snow was melting under the hot sun, leaving all the paths slippery to walk on.

All through the journey, Majila's thoughts returned to the fire and his last look at Aalym. She was his life and without her he knew every day would be a struggle. He knew he had to be strong for Esmee though, so he would be, but in those moments he had to himself the tears would flow. They had been walking for hours when they finally reached the foothills of the mountains. Majila stopped to rest; in the distance, he could see buildings. From where he stood, it looked like a small city with a monastery looming above everything else. His spirits rose and he started forward again.

'Not long now, Esmee my love. We will have food and shelter. We will be safe, I promise you.'

Majila hoped that this was true as he started walking towards the city. Esmee held his shoulders tight, her green eyes lit up and she smiled as she spoke one word: 'Safe.'

CHAPTER 7

Black Wolf awoke early, his mind racing with his dream. He reached for his box and pulled out the journal that Grey Moon had given him. Using a piece of charcoal, he quickly wrote down everything about the dream that he could recall. Just like the fire, this was so vivid that he was certain it must mean something. He had to see Grey Moon, but didn't want to wake him too early, so he decided to get himself ready for the day and then set out to speak to his friend.

Grey Moon was already awake in his hut; he too had dreamt during the night and had woken early to plan for the journey he'd soon be taking. Grey Moon spoke to the spirits alone in his hut; he needed to know what was happening, because his dream had shaken him so much. His hut was filled with smoke from the herbs he was burning, the sweet scent filling his nose and heightening all of his senses. He clutched his ancient beads and rocked slowly, chanting a language long forgotten since the days of old. Slowly, words and visions appeared to him as the spirits guided his every move. The words came out of Grey Moon's mouth without any effort on his behalf:

'There is a great danger present. Its cloak of darkness surrounds the wall of man. The fate of one power is out of your hands but they will find you. Only then can you search for the other half. He must be told the mark of his creation but very little else. You are wise, Grey Moon, and all you have seen alone is true. He who is of you, starts and ends the circle.'

Then the words were gone and Grey Moon opened his eyes. The thick smoke funnelled into a line and was sucked backwards towards the burning herbs, extinguishing the flame the moment they touched it. Then the hut was empty, and not even a hint of the smoke's beautiful smell remained. He would sit with Black Wolf and make the plans that were needed. This journey was starting today.

Black Wolf turned over the dream in his mind as he made it to Grey Moon's hut. He felt close to understanding the pieces of the puzzle but still so far from solving it. Grey Moon was covering his hut just as Black Wolf arrived.

'Morning, my friend, we have lots to plan today. If we go

to the shelter of the woods we can talk in private without any risk of disturbance.'

Black Wolf agreed, so together they headed off to the woods.

'I had another vision last night, Grey Moon. The fire was all but gone and I was trekking. I had a child with me and we were headed for safety together. I felt it was the next part of my story, if that makes sense?'

Black Wolf was embarrassed at speaking so profoundly but it was the only way he could explain what he had seen in his sleep.

'It makes perfect sense, my child. You have also taken the first step to understanding these visions too; you have put yourself in the centre. It is through your eyes that you see and now the story can flow more easily.'

Grey Moon smiled to himself; he could feel that his young friend was learning quickly.

'I've never dreamt like that before. The landscape and the situation seems familiar to me but in a strange way. Like being told a story as an old man and recognising it vaguely from childhood. I don't know who I am in the dream but the child's face I cannot seem to forget, even when I'm awake. Is she haunting me?'

Grey Moon shook his head, still smiling. 'We haunt ourselves, my friend. Nothing more, nothing less. You are very close to realising the most important part of your dreams and I'm sure you will find the rest easily enough. Keep writing and in the moments of reflection, use your senses and find what feels right. Remember, nothing has to be proven for it to be true. We live surrounded by many truths that are hidden within fables. You are doing well, so try not to get disheartened. Keep breathing and trust in what your heart knows is true.'

Black Wolf was deep in thought and before he knew it, they had reached a small clearing in the woods. Huge trees stood round in a circle, like guards on duty, and in the centre of the clearing was a big hollowed-out tree stump. Half was filled with moss and leaves, leaving the top open to the elements. Black Wolf looked around and fought back the rising emotions as he spoke: 'Is this where I was found as a child?'

Grey Moon looked into the tree stump. His brow creased

as he seemed to get lost for a moment, staring into the deep, empty space. 'Yes, my child. This is where you came from when you were brought to the camp. It was snowing that night and the traveller walked out of the woods with you in his arms. The world around looked grey, except for your deep brown eyes. I thought this would be a good place to talk. You entered our camp from here and this will be the last place we sit before leaving here tomorrow. It seemed fitting to draw the circle.'

Black Wolf looked around at everything in amazement, trying to imagine the huge surroundings from a child's view. He looked carefully at the tree stump and could see the claw marks that the wolf had left behind when it stood protecting him. He placed his palm over the prints and tears welled up in his eyes. His family, all here. The woods serving as his mother and a wolf, his father. He felt lost and found in this same moment. He was ready to find his destiny.

Grey Moon had laid down a rug for them and Black Wolf sat, his back resting against the tree stump. The sense of pride he finally felt from seeing this place gave him more strength than ever before.

'I need to talk to you about the mark of your creation and I thought this place would be the most natural setting for our discussions.' Grey Moon grew serious as he worked through just how much he should tell Black Wolf and how much he had to discover alone.

'I have heard this mentioned in old fables, but never has it been explained to me, Grey Moon.'

'As I said earlier, Wolf, lots of truths lie hidden behind fables. The mark of your creation is something that all people have. Our elders believe it to be the wound by which you left your last world and appears on your skin as you enter the next. No one is sure why, but our ancestors believed it to be a sort of spiritual gift to remind us all that we've existed before. They also believed that the powers, which have always existed, are special. The mark of creation has an even greater meaning for the chosen ones, and the leader of men.'

Black Wolf touched his right eye. Deep in the innermost corner lay his mark of creation. He'd heard stories regarding these marks when he was a child but never had he known any to be true. He remembered some of the elders used to be fascinated by his mark and talk amongst themselves about it but never to him.

'So what does this mean for me, Grey Moon? Can you explain more?'

Grey Moon looked deep into his young friend's eyes, and spoke: 'You left your last world through that mark. You died as a result of an injury deep where that mark lies. As you are the leader of men, it's important that I reveal something to you. Through all the battles you fought as a young warrior, did you ever wonder why you left them with nothing but cuts and bruises? Great men fell all around you but you stood strong and always returned safely. Why is that?'

Black Wolf thought about his early struggles in battle; some had been very vicious before the peace that his people now had. Through all the fights he had remained safe, despite standing alone and entering battles with a reckless heart.

'What are you saying, Grey Moon? I don't understand. You aren't telling me I cannot die, surely?'

'As the leader of men, you will age like any other and if you fall ill you will become sick and weak like any other. But the spirits declared many ages ago that the mark of creation would be the only way to kill the chosen one before his time. Every gift gets passed on, but only once the person truly understands that gift. You will get old like me and eventually die, but to remove you before your time is up would take a weapon struck into your mark of creation. Without that, you would be merely injured but still alive.'

Black Wolf stood quickly. What Grey Moon had said made perfect sense in such a strange way. All his cuts and bruises had healed throughout his life; he had never suffered any worse than that.

'I know this is a great deal to follow and understand, my child. I spoke to the spirits earlier today and I was told that you must know this. I don't want to confuse you or make your journey harder. I am here to try to help guide you on your way. The rest you must do yourself.'

Black Wolf looked down at Grey Moon. He seemed so old and frail yet so young and strong at the same time. 'Who are you, Grey Moon?'

Grey Moon glanced up and caught Black Wolf's deep brown eyes, trying to hide the tears welling up as he spoke. 'You should think of me as merely a traveller, Black Wolf.'

CHAPTER 8

In Orgent, Amelia was sat in the kitchen talking to Elspeth. All around her, the staff hurried about, preparing recipes and planning food. After her day in the market, Amelia had been thinking about her father and how deeply he'd been studying his paperwork. She knew that if she asked him he'd tell her nothing, so she glanced at the papers while he was busy, and found plans for a big celebration within the city's walls that very night. As controlling as her father was, he often surprised her with such occasions. She thought he still saw her as his little girl and that surprise parties would mean a lot to her. In truth, Amelia wanted to know in advance so she could prepare what to wear and the anticipation would give her something real to break the monotony of her caged life. She didn't want to upset her father, though, so she was pretending to have no idea of the party and was carrying on as normal.

'Amelia, you really need to leave the kitchen soon. If your father comes in to check on the food then he will know you are already aware of the surprise.'

Elspeth loved Amelia dearly, but found her stubborn streak difficult to deal with at such times.

'I cannot sit in my room for a whole day though, Elspeth. You know how mad it drives me, sitting up there, watching everything happen to all but me.'

'I do know how you feel, but we mustn't spoil this for your father. We must go!' With this, Elspeth pulled the princess by the hand through the backdoor of the kitchen and out into the small garden at the back of the temple.

Amelia liked sitting here, surrounded by all the beautiful flowers, and with the sun so warm today she decided there were worse places she could be.

Upstairs in the study, the head of the guards was in discussion with the emperor.

'I appreciate your trouble guarding the city when the gates are open, but this party will need them open so we can make room for all the celebrations.'

The emperor had been studying the city's plans and though he never liked opening the gate, he'd decided it was the only way that the party could work. He had planned fireworks to close the event and it was far too dangerous with the great doors closed. So he had made a plan, which involved opening them just for the end, working out that the smoke would hide the gates being open anyway.

'I know you have gone to great lengths for this party, Emperor. I just fear that it will leave us exposed and that is always a worry for my men and me. If this is your wish though, I assure you it will be done.'

The head guard knew that challenging the emperor was pointless and decided that instead of arguing, he would spend the rest of the day making sure the guards were ready for any problems.

'Thank you, my friend. You have served me loyally for many years. I understand your concerns but your men are watching every night and see no threat of attack. The wild animals outside the city walls haven't been a problem to us for a long time and the sickness is also controlled now. I'm sure we have nothing to fear. Tell your men to be vigilant and everything will be fine.'

The emperor stood, signalling the end of the discussion. Slowly the head guard also stood, bowed, and made his way out of the room.

'Any problems, let me know and we can sort them out before this event.'

'I will, Emperor, thank you.'

With the conversation over, the emperor closed the door. The head guard started making his way back to speak to his men and give them their orders. Walking down the steps of the temple, he was troubled at the thought of opening the gates. For the past few nights he had increased security at the wall and despite his men seeing nothing strange, he himself had an odd feeling. He couldn't prove anything but had a sense that there was something outside the city walls and it left him feeling very uneasy about the planned celebrations.

CHAPTER 9

Deep in the mountains, north-east of Orgent, Lone Wolf sat alone in his cave. He had been out hunting all morning and had finally returned with enough food to last him a few days. As he skinned the carcasses of his hunting victories, he saw a brief movement in the rocks ahead of him. He watched as a black wolf walked out of its hiding place and stood staring directly at him. The wolf had appeared out of nowhere for the last couple of days now and after a short time, had disappeared again without a trace.

'I don't know what it is you want, but there must be a reason why you keep appearing? Are you a loner like me? Or maybe you're just hungry?'

Lone Wolf threw some meat for the wolf and watched as it passed right through him. Stunned, Lone Wolf jumped to his feet and ran out onto the mountain ledge. The meat was lying in the dirt and the wolf was nowhere to be seen.

He left the meat where it was and walked back to his cave; it hadn't occurred to him before that he'd been visited by a spirit animal. Suddenly the air felt cold around him and a chill ran down his spine, so he lit a small fire and continued preparing his food, feeling a little more apprehensive than before.

Lone Wolf had lived in the mountains for years now. He had once been part of a tribe who had lived far from the area in which he now dwelt. In those times, there was no peace amongst any of the settlers though and wars often broke out. Having lost his parents in one of the many violent battles long ago, he had decided to walk away from the tribe and live his life alone somewhere quiet. He had trekked for weeks before arriving at these mountains and it took days further before he found a suitable place to stay. Eventually he found a cave and although it wasn't that big, there was more than enough room for him to live in alone. Everything he needed was around him; he could hunt for food and there were lots of fruit and vegetables growing naturally in the wooded areas nearby. It took him a little time to get used to this new way of life, but once he had he found it a lot more enjoyable than the tribes, with their battles and constant moving. The only thing he had brought with him from those days was his belief in ancient arts and customs. During his time with the tribe, he had been taught many things, including meditation using fire, and this was one practice that he still used regularly.

Having finished sorting his food he sat looking into the heart of his campfire. The flames twisted and turned around each other, dancing as one and then separating again. He relaxed and let his mind quieten, feeling the warmth of the flames spread from his toes and slowly up his body. In his mind, he saw the flames separate again and take shape. Two figures moved towards another and joined together, creating one strong-looking frame. A third figure stood separate from them, and in the distance he saw the sky turn blacker than he had ever seen before. The only noise was the single call of a wolf. As the image slowly faded and turned back into flames, he opened his eyes and knew what it all meant.

He moved back into the cave and made as much room as he could. Soon he would be having visitors, he was sure.

CHAPTER 10

Black Wolf and Grey Moon returned to their camp. There were things to be done before they started their journey and there was no time to waste. Grey Moon had headed to talk to some of the elders to see if they could assemble a small group of warriors together, should they be needed. He also had to warn them to be vigilant as the camp itself would soon be a target if things went wrong.

Black Wolf was back at his hut, packing the supplies they needed for their journey. Grey Moon had told him of certain essentials they required but also that they'd have to travel fairly lightly in order to move quickly when needed. He had packed some food, the hunting bag, a couple of skins and a fur blanket. The last item he had to pack was the box that Grey Moon had given him. He opened it to check that the book was in there. It was, and he slowly flicked through its pages. The dreams of fire and trekking played out in his mind and he felt so close to realising what they meant, but something was holding him back. The one thing he couldn't forget was the girl's face though, so he grabbed his charcoal and drew her on the page next to where he'd written that dream. The picture came out perfectly and as he stared at those familiar features, something inside him felt pain like never before. As he sat, staring at the face, he heard a woman's voice speaking to him: 'You must save Esmee.'

Black Wolf looked outside his tent but there was no one there. The voice had been so familiar to him though and felt strangely comforting. With his charcoal, he wrote the name Esmee below the picture and continued to look at it. Who was this girl and why did she feature so prominently in his dreams?

He was sure that there was a connection between him and this girl with the haunting green eyes, but he didn't know any more than that. He put the book back in the box and packed it in his sack. The sack was quite heavy so he had tied rope to it, enabling him to wear it on his back. When he hoisted it onto his shoulders he felt that strange familiarity once more. He took one last look in his hut and sealed it shut; he wasn't sure if or when he would be back here again.

Grey Moon had finished talking to the other elders and they had agreed to his requests. A group of twenty men would train and prepare themselves for battle if needed. He had told them that there would be a sign if they were to come and help, but that he wasn't sure what the sign would be. They would know though, he had reassured them. The elders had wished him well on his journey and had started to search for their warriors. Grey Moon packed his spirit herbs and nothing else. He was confident that Black Wolf would bring everything they needed, so he sealed his hut and sat waiting for his friend to join him. Grey Moon watched as the tribe carried on their routines as normal; nothing had changed for them and he hoped it wouldn't have to. This battle wasn't theirs and all he could wish for was, with Black Wolf's leadership, they could keep everyone safe from harm.

Black Wolf arrived at Grey Moon's hut a short while later.

'I've got everything you asked for here and am ready to start our journey.'

Grey Moon glanced up at his friend and forced a smile, yet his eyes gave away his worries. 'I'm not sure any of us are ready, my child, but you are starting to look like the man of strength that you truly are. I have spoken to the elders and they will gather some fighters for us should we need them. I guess it's now time to say goodbye to this land and start our journey. We have far to travel, so let's begin.'

Grey Moon reached out his hand and Black Wolf helped pull him to his feet.

'Where are we going, Grey Moon?'

Black Wolf was eager to start their journey before his spirit started to weaken.

'First we must head into the mountains. It will take days to get there and we will stop to rest before we reach them. Remember that the spirits told us we would be joined by another before starting our quest, once they arrive then we will move quickly and be closer to reaching our goal.'

Black Wolf was desperate to have more answers but knew that he'd get them before long. One thing still troubled him though. 'How will this other person know where to find us, Grey Moon?'

Grey Moon had quietly pondered the same question

and the only answer he could give Black Wolf was what he believed was true: 'Fate has set in motion a series of events, Wolf. We may not like it or understand why, but these things are happening and now we must follow the paths that become clear to us. All we can hope for is that others do the same and our mother helps the four powers to reunite. Have faith, child. We will be joined before too long by an important visitor, and then we can search for the others. This journey will be hard for you in many ways but remember the advice I give you and you will see the truth. Let's go now — we have much to do.'

Grey Moon gently guided Black Wolf forward and the two began heading out of the camp. Grey Moon's mind filled with many visions as he walked. He hoped that Black Wolf was ready for this and that he would deal with what he learned on this journey as painlessly as possible. This man, with such a past and such a future. Grey Moon looked at him and choked back the tears that stung his eyes. He would not lose him again.

CHAPTER 11

The sun had burned itself out and now, as it had started to set for the night to come rushing in, the sky above Orgent was a dark, almost blackened, shade of blue.

The emperor had found Amelia in the gardens earlier and had given her the big surprise. Amelia had used her talents to the full in order to fake shock and excitement before embracing her father, who soon became flustered and left her to prepare.

Sitting in his study, watching the sky darken, the emperor was very excited about his big finale for the party. He had time to relax now as he knew everything was being taken care of; his daughter had been so shocked at the announcement of the event, so he could watch time move by with a satisfied smile on his face. He hadn't thrown a party in quite a while now and was determined that tonight would be remembered for a long time.

Amelia was in her room with Elspeth, frantically looking through her clothes. She was desperate to find something really special to wear and was running out of time.

'It will be a cold night, Amelia, so you need something practical as well as attractive.' Elspeth often sounded like a mother, but the last thing she needed was to be looking after an ill princess who was grumpy.

'I cannot find anything yet, Elspeth, so I'll be lucky to even attend. I wish I'd known sooner, then I could've had something made specially.'

Elspeth watched as clothing flew through the air and landed, scattered, all around her. Suddenly an idea sprang into her mind.

'What about your mother's clothes? There were many parties back then and I'm sure she'd have some lovely outfits. Maybe you could wear one of them? I've seen them all in the spare room and I'm sure most of them would fit you perfectly.'

Amelia stopped rummaging through her clothes immediately and turned to Elspeth.

'That's a wonderful idea. You know I won't go into that room, but you can. Find something that will look perfect and I'll wear that. I trust you to choose well — you've never let me down before. You'd better go now though, time is short if I'm to be ready for tonight!'

Elspeth stood up and made her way carefully through the clothes lying scattered on the floor. 'I will be as quick as I can, Amelia, then we must do your hair. Don't worry, we'll be ready in time, I promise.'

As Elspeth left the room, Amelia started tidying away all the piles of clothes. She felt a lot more positive about the party now and was ready to have as much fun as she could.

Inside the walls of Orgent, people were busy setting out everything for the party. In the big open courtyard, tables had been arranged into a huge square. There was a separate line of tables for the emperor, princess and other special people from the temple. The whole city had been cleaned from head to toe and now decorations were being hung up, making the city fit for a huge celebration. Night was soon approaching, so lanterns were lit and the city glowed beautifully beneath the darkening sky. The food was ready and there was an army of servants ready to give everyone their meals. In a short time, the party would start and the city would be awaiting the arrival of its emperor and his daughter.

High above the city, the guards were continuing their checks to make sure everything was safe. The unease at opening the gates had dwindled throughout the day and the guards were looking forward to enjoying the celebrations like everyone else. The head guard still couldn't shake off his strange feeling though and was determined that he would be the one opening the gates, rather than leaving it to one of his men. He was pacing back and forth by the gates, checking all the plans in his head and making sure he was prepared for anything. To him the sky seemed darker than usual and he struggled to escape the cold wind that seemingly appeared from nowhere. He pulled his collar up higher, stuck his hands deep into his pockets and continued pacing, his breath forming ghostly wisps in the cold night air.

Outside Orgent, it was even darker. The lack of lights and the cover from the trees created vast black areas at the foot of the city's walls. Under the cover of this darkness there was an even blacker gathering. One large mass split into many, first just a few but before long, hundreds. These dark figures moved without a sound, always remaining hidden. The shapes continued to change, from small to large, human forms became animals and back again. Directly in front of the gates, stood beneath a huge tree, completely cloaked in darkness, was the largest of the shadowy figures. In a voice that hissed out of him like cold air, he spoke one sentence.

'It is time.'

CHAPTER 12

Black Wolf and Grey Moon had reached the river where they had fished previously. On their journey, they had watched as the sky had grown darker above them. The once blue sky was now nearly black and they knew it wouldn't be long before they'd have to stop for the night. Beneath the dark sky, the river looked much wider than it had done in daylight. Pockets of shadow scattered around and made it difficult to see what was earth and what was water. Black Wolf had put down his sack and was refreshing himself by splashing the cool water of the river on his face and neck. In the darkness, he couldn't rely on just his sight, so his other senses were working twice as hard to make him aware of his surroundings. He could hear every twig snap and every rustle of leaves as all the animals in the woods went about their lives, and he could smell the rich fragrances of all the different vegetation around him.

As he dried his hands on his cloak, he felt a cool chill appear from nowhere and blow through him. He shivered and turned towards where Grey Moon stood, looking grave.

'Do you feel how cold it is getting? Why do I feel like something's changed?'

Grey Moon nodded silently in agreement. 'The darkness is upon us, child. It seems everything is moving quicker than I expected. That cold is born of the evil that hopes to choke the life out of us all. You feel this and it unsettles you, for you are the centre of all our lives. I fear we may not have much time, my child. We need to cross the river tonight and get to the mountains before nightfall tomorrow.'

Black Wolf wrapped his cloak tighter around him and stared into the waters of the river. On a hot day he would gladly dive into it and enjoy the cool water washing over him, but he wasn't sure he could even manage to stand in it if this cold wind kept blowing through.

'I've never been beyond this riverbank before, Grey Moon. Can we even cross it? It's so wide and must be deep...'

'Trust me, I've crossed this river many times, my child. It will be warmer than you think, for it is only the air that is chilled by the evil surrounding us. If you walk through the water with your arms held high, your chest will be above the water level and everything you have packed will stay dry. The bed is very smooth so you have little fear of tripping. I will go first, if you wish? Follow my path and we will soon be on the other side.'

Black Wolf watched as Grey Moon held his small bag high above his head and stepped into the river. The water did stop at his chest and he seemed to have no problem walking across to the other side.

'The water is actually warmer than the air. Follow me and we can soon find a place to stop and get dry.'

Grey Moon had called over his shoulder without stopping. Steadily, he carried on walking across without any distraction at all. In the light reflecting off the water, Grey Moon had an almost silver glow around him and Black Wolf thought that he looked every bit the magical man he was rumoured to be. It made him wonder just how much Grey Moon already knew about these events. Shaking the daydreams from his head, he picked up his sack and held it high in the air as he too stepped into the dark waters. Despite the cold air, which was still inexplicably chilling him to the core, he found the temperature of the water quite bearable. He wouldn't have said it was warm, but it certainly wasn't as cold as he had originally feared. Grey Moon had already made it to the other side and was doing his best to wring out any water from his clothing. He was stood in quite a large clearing between the forest and the river, big enough for a small fire, and he decided that was exactly what they needed.

'Keep moving steadily, Wolf. I think we should stop for a short while. I will light a fire so we can both dry out properly before moving on.'

Black Wolf liked the sound of being warm and dry again, and had to stop himself from running through the water for fear of tripping and falling in completely. He knew he couldn't afford to get any of his belongings wet, so he carried on moving slowly.

'Please do, Grey Moon, I look forward to being dry again and to be warm as well would be very welcome. I won't be much longer.'

Black Wolf carried on moving towards the other side as his friend went about collecting wood for the fire. By the time he had made it to the other side the fire was already burning brightly. Grey Moon sat next to it, watching the steam rise from his clothing as it slowly dried.

'What took you so long, child?' Grey Moon chuckled to himself as he witnessed the look of surprise on Black Wolf's face.

'You never fail to amaze me, Grey Moon. Not only have you managed to gather wood for a fire, but you already have it burning and are drying out, whilst I'm here soaking wet.'

It was true, the speed with which Grey Moon was able to do things often surprised Black Wolf. He could only hope that by spending more time together, he too could learn to be so skilled.

'It's always nice to surprise people. Come, sit and dry out, we have much walking to do before we stop tonight.'

Grey Moon looked quite pleased at impressing Black Wolf. He started planning the next stages of their journey in his head.

Black Wolf sat down and opened his sack. He was starting to feel hungry and figured he'd better eat now as they probably wouldn't be stopping again soon. As he delved into his sack to find some food, he spotted a faint reddish glow coming from inside. Nervously, he found the source of the light: it was the box Grey Moon had given him. Quickly, he removed the box and placed it by the fire, between the two of them.

Black Wolf looked on with wonder; one of the four carvings, the picture of a rock, was glowing brightly. It was a deep, reddish brown colour and was seemingly lit from nowhere.

'Grey Moon, look. What's happening to the box you gave me? It's glowing, how is this possible?'

Grey Moon smiled to himself as he answered. 'Many truths are brought to life by the power of our mother herself, child. Nature can hide truths but it can also reveal them. It seems now is the time for you to learn more — she has spoken.'

Black Wolf sat silently, desperate to learn more about everything that was happening around him.

'As I told you before, my child, that box has been with me for years. Before that, it was with my own tribe's elders for years, and the same before that. It has always been our duty to look after it until its rightful owners appeared. On the box is the marking of our mother, the eye that sees all and watches over us. In the four corners are the symbols of her four main special children, the powerful ones that I have spoken of before. The stories tell that only the box can truly reveal who those four are and it will show them by illuminating that symbol, to help them see. It glows for you, my child; you are one of the four. The rock, our mother's most loyal son. Born of the earth and born to lead the Earth. It is you, my child.'

Black Wolf traced his finger over the carving; the glow was strongest when he touched the box. 'What am I to do with the box though? Where are the others?'

'You will guard the box, child. When the four are together, you will know what to do with it. This journey we are making must unite all four of you, or I fear it will all be too late. Trust your instincts; we are on the right path.'

Everything Grey Moon said made sense to Black Wolf, even though part of him didn't want to believe it. He carefully placed the box back in the sack and moved closer to the fire. Soon steam was filling the air as they both dried out.

'I am ready when you are, Black Wolf.'

Grey Moon got to his feet and stretched out ready for their long trek. Whilst he waited for Black Wolf, he picked up a thick branch and lit the end, giving them a torch for their journey into the forest.

'Let's get going then. I am ready too.'

Grey Moon held out his hand and pulled Black Wolf to his feet, where he then hoisted his sack onto his back and stamped out the remainder of the fire. Once they were ready, the two men began walking towards the thick forest and the darkness beyond.

The walk through the forest was made a lot easier by the glowing embers of the branch that Grey Moon carried, but it was still awkward to manoeuvre in such tight spaces. The woods surrounding their camp had been thinned out by the natives when collecting firewood but the woodland here was left untouched, making it very dense and tricky to move through. Grey Moon was being careful not to set the forest alight, whilst Black Wolf used a knife to clear an easier path for them. During their trek, Black Wolf's mind was thinking about everything the last few days had brought him. He had always wished to be more than just another of the natives, going through their lives without excitement, but he wasn't sure if all this hope and faith in him wasn't misguided. How could anyone follow him when he had no idea where he was meant to go?

'The trick is not to think too much, my child. You have more questions than answers I know, but trust me, it will come together and then you will face a decision.'

Grey Moon's voice had broken the silence and again he seemed to know what Black Wolf was thinking.

'How do you do that, Grey Moon? It's like you can hear my thoughts.' Black Wolf wanted to know if this was another skill he could learn or whether it was something that only Grey Moon could do, like many of his talents appeared to be.

'I've spent a long time watching, listening and speaking to people. Over time you realise that most things are easy to see with a bit of awareness. It is no trick or magic that I use; I have merely learnt how people think. With age you will learn so much, my friend, and you will see what I see. Your worries are loud enough for the whole forest to hear, but I assure you it is nothing to fear. When the time is right, you will know what to do.'

Despite any doubts, Black Wolf found Grey Moon's faith in him reassuring. He trusted Grey Moon completely and that gave him the strength he needed to follow his path, wherever it led.

They had been trekking for quite some time when Black Wolf noticed how much the forest had thinned out. In the flickering light of the burning embers, he saw glimpses of grey through the trees.

'We are nearly there, child — the mountains are within reach. We should find shelter at the foot of their huge frame and then early tomorrow we must move on.'

Black Wolf was glad they were stopping soon. He hadn't travelled so far before and was feeling both hungry and tired. As they walked, he watched the forest slowly fall away until they made it to an open plain. Behind the plain stood the foot of the huge mountains; looking up, they were so tall that Black Wolf couldn't even see the top. The dark night sky seemed to swallow the rock face halfway up and hide the rest from view. It was a spectacular sight and Black Wolf knew that looking at it in the morning would be a moment he'd never forget.

'There's a shallow cave at the bottom over there that we can use to rest tonight, Wolf. In the morning we will need to move fast; we don't know exactly how much time we have. If you collect some wood we can have a fire and warm ourselves before we settle down for the night.'

Grey Moon walked over to the cliff face while Black Wolf collected some fallen branches from the edge of the forest. He was desperate to get warm again and then rest before continuing tomorrow. As he stood at the edge of the forest, he once again heard the noises of all the animals around him. Each tiny sound reminded him that life goes on, regardless of everything happening around it.

Black Wolf had a heavy load of wood and dropped it at the foot of the mountains where Grey Moon was waiting for him. The cave was big enough for the two of them to sleep in but had room for little else. He didn't care though, as long as he had warmth and shelter. Grey Moon arranged the wood for a fire and packed dry leaves he'd found underneath the pile. Then with a touch of his smouldering branch, it caught light and started to burn away. Within minutes they could both feel the heat starting to rise and were settled down next to it, letting the warmth seep into their aching bodies.

'You need to sleep soon, my child. Tomorrow we must make it up the mountains. We will find another there who can help us. If we move quickly when it's light then we can be there before half the day is gone.'

Black Wolf watched as Grey Moon spread the blankets inside the opening of the cave. He had left Black Wolf's sack open when he'd removed the blankets, and once again there was a glow illuminating from within.

'Can we leave the fire burning, Grey Moon? Or do we need to put it out?' Black Wolf was worried about attracting any unwanted attention before they reached their destination and he knew that they could easily be attacked whilst they slept.

'Leave it to burn out, Wolf. The evil will not come to us; in fact, it is waiting for us to go to it. We are safe here.'

Grey Moon settled down in his blankets, searching for the radiance that had caught his eye before. Black Wolf noticed his friend's interest and pulled the box out of the bag, expecting to see the rock symbol still glowing. He gasped as he noticed that, while the symbol was indeed still lit, it had now been joined by another glimmer. This time the symbol representing wind was glowing blue. However, it was not a steady source of light like the symbol for rock; it was flickering.

'It's another symbol, Grey Moon. The wind! Why is it glowing like that though? It's different, what does that mean?'

Grey Moon settled down under his blankets and closed his eyes, his breath even as he spoke calmly. 'You need to sleep now, child. That is the second of the special ones. The flickering can only mean one thing: she is coming.'

CHAPTER 13

Whilst Black Wolf and Grey Moon had been on their journey, Orgent had been alive like never before. The celebrations had been going all night, with the population making the most of the event their emperor had created for them. It had all started quite quietly with a large feast. All the people had sat down and waited for the arrival of the emperor and his daughter, Princess Amelia. When they had finally descended the steep steps of the temple and entered the courtyard, all the people stood to welcome them and looked on in awe. The emperor looked immaculate in his finest robes, the gold edgings just adding to the authority that he already had. His daughter Amelia followed closely behind and drew gasps from everyone watching. She was wearing the most beautiful dress, as blue as a summer sky and shimmering under the night-lights. The dress made her eyes look bluer than usual and a combination of the two made her look like an angel who had flown down to light up Orgent like never before. Some of the older people amongst the population realised that the dress had once been her mother's and were stunned that Amelia could eclipse her mother's beauty so easily, but she did. She truly was a princess and they felt honoured just to be in her company.

The emperor had been shocked when he saw Amelia's choice of outfit for the party but had always known deep down that the day would come when his daughter took his wife's place as the most beautiful lady in Orgent. He had been quite emotional when he saw her but had given his full blessing and was proud of the woman she had become. During the feast, the emperor had lost himself in memories. Seeing Amelia in his wife's dress had brought many daydreams flooding back and he struggled to maintain any conversation whilst being so deep in thought. Amelia had spent the meal chatting excitedly to Elspeth about the fireworks and music that would signal the main part of the celebrations, but was troubled by the faraway look in her father's eyes. She assumed that, despite his blessing, it was because of her outfit and hoped she hadn't caused him any pain by choosing it. Once the feast was eaten, the servants hurried to clear all the tables before more men came and folded them away, leaving the whole courtyard open for the dancing that was next to start.

The emperor had cornered his head guard and discussed the plan regarding the fireworks and opening of Orgent's gates.

'Everything is in place, Emperor. When the music ends we will open the gates and the fireworks will be lit, then when finished we will close the gates and clear up in daylight.'

The emperor had so many thoughts running through his head and barely heard his guard.

'I've changed my mind — I want the fireworks before the end. I have decided we will have the royal dance, then the fireworks and then finish with more music for all the people to dance to.'

Surprised by the sudden change of plan, the guard's anxiety suddenly increased. 'But we aren't prepared for that, Emperor... My men have it all planned for the end of the celebrations.'

'I suggest you change the plan quickly then. I have people to talk to and cannot stand around here all night discussing this. When the first part of the dancing ends, I will give you a signal and will be expecting the fireworks. If you need to consult with your men then do it now, but do it quickly; the dancing and music will be starting soon.'

The emperor turned abruptly and headed back to the festivities, leaving the head guard standing alone. He felt a surge of anger at the emperor's sharp reaction and was shocked at the sudden change of plan. For all his years working for the emperor, he had never known him to be anything but courteous and very methodical in his planning, yet tonight he seemed agitated and troubled. The head guard marched off to his men. He had a plan to alter — and fast.

Whilst her father had been busy with the head guard, Amelia had been mixing with the population of Orgent. Looking like a princess but acting like every other person was something that came naturally to her. The position she held within the city had never rested easily on her shoulders, and she preferred to be one of the people and be free to talk naturally rather than have any authority. Nights like this were the perfect opportunity for her to feel normal and be relaxed enough to talk to anyone on an equal level. The only thing that caused any problems for her was how she was dressed; she would've preferred to blend in far more. Amelia had arranged a solution to this though, and with Elspeth's help she had hidden a sack containing a dark, hooded cape near the main doors of Orgent. She could slip it over her dress later and be free to mingle with the crowds, happily looking a lot more like a normal person. As Amelia wandered through the crowd, she caught sight of her father walking sternly away from the head guard and managed to catch up with him.

'Are you okay, Father? You seem so very serious tonight and I'm worried about you. I hope I haven't done anything to upset you?'

The emperor stopped and put his hands on his daughter's cheeks. 'Of course not, my child. Seeing you in your mother's dress made me realise how much you've grown up and brought back many memories, but that's not a bad thing. You look beautiful and I'm so proud of you. I have lots to arrange with these events though and sometimes it causes me trouble, but I promise you, I am fine. The music will start soon and we must open the dancing, then I want you to enjoy the rest of your night!'

Amelia felt comforted that there wasn't anything wrong and walked with her father through the crowd. They stopped and spoke to many of the people but everyone was then quietened by the sound of drums, signalling the start of the music.

Everyone moved quietly to the sides of the courtyard, forming a large open space framed by the population of Orgent. The emperor walked slowly to the centre of the open space and addressed the crowd.

'People of Orgent, I welcome you all to our gathering tonight. It is wonderful to see so many of you all enjoying the party. We have eaten well and I'd like to thank everyone who has helped make this such a special occasion. We will now enjoy some gentle music and will then finish the night dancing and drinking in a way that's worthy of an Orgent party. So to start the dance, I'd like to invite my daughter, your princess, Amelia, to join me for the first dance.'

The crowds stood clapping as Amelia made her way to the centre and took her father's hand. The slow music began and the two royal figures moved softly beneath the night sky. Time seemed to stop for the people of Orgent and they stood transfixed as two of their finest icons moved with grace and beauty around the square. It reminded the older generations of the emperor and his wife many years ago, while the younger generation were witnessing what would one day be a golden memory to them.

At the end of the dance, all the people of Orgent applauded the two royal figures with an excitement that hadn't been seen for many years. In the middle of the square, the emperor embraced Amelia and spoke softly in her ear. 'You bring me such happiness and I am so proud of you, Amelia. You should go and enjoy the rest of the evening now and I will see you when it's all finished.'

Amelia kissed her father on the cheek and said, 'I love you, Father, and always will.'

Then she slipped quietly into the crowd and headed towards her hidden sack. The emperor stood alone in the square surrounded by all his people and addressed the crowd once more: 'People of Orgent, the music will begin again shortly, but first I wish to thank everyone for the effort they've put in tonight, making it such a special occasion. I hand over to all of you now, for this is your time. We will see the fireworks and then the rest of the night you shall dance away.'

Once again, the crowd applauded as the emperor signalled to the guards at the gate and moved through the crowd, back towards the temple. He had decided earlier to watch the fireworks from here and then retire to the temple, leaving the people of Orgent to carry on enjoying the night their own way. On his way to the temple, he caught Elspeth's attention and asked her if she could fetch him a drink once the fireworks had ended.

'I can get it for you now, Emperor, it's not any trouble. The fireworks will be so loud anyway and sometimes the bangs scare me.'

So Elspeth went in search of a drink for the emperor, softly disappearing into the temple. The guards had seen the emperor's signal and started to open the gates of Orgent. They made a loud rumbling noise as they were opened, causing the people to look in awe as the city opened itself to the world outside. As the gates rumbled open, the head guard kept watch nervously, ready to ignite the fireworks and then close the gates again as soon as he could.

Whilst the fireworks were wheeled towards the entrance, Amelia seized her opportunity and pulled the long dark cloak over her, making her almost invisible in the dark night. She watched as the great gates were opened, staring at the dense black sky outside. In the dark, she could barely make out the shapes of the trees and slowly stepped back into the shadow of the wall, transfixed by the freedom she'd always longed for.

The fireworks were in place and the head guard lit the main fuse. They were designed to be lit together but some fuses burnt a lot slower than others so, instead of igniting together, they would form a pattern one after the other, creating a wonderful display. One by one they flew up into the air and exploded. The people cheered with delight, watching all the colours burning vividly in the black sky. The last was the biggest of all, and as the colourful sparks showered down over Orgent there was a huge explosion, making the ground shudder beneath everyone's feet. The smoke billowed out, filling the entrance to the city, and the emperor slowly turned and made his way up the temple steps, satisfied that the evening had passed successfully. Before the guards could move to douse the dying flames of the firework, a second loud explosion shook everyone to the floor and they watched in horror as a huge shadowy figure emerged from the smoke.

'Stay on your knees, Orgent, or a far worse fate will come to you. Running or fighting is useless and any who try will perish where they stand,' the loud voice boomed out.

As the figure emerged from the smoke, the guards rushed at it with their weapons, ready to attack the stranger. From the side of where the smoke appeared, Amelia watched as eight guards charged angrily at the figure who, holding an open palm to them, caused them all to drop where they were. She stifled a cry as the fallen men crumbled to dust before her eyes until there was nothing left of them.

'Let that serve as a warning to you all. No one can defeat me; it is pointless to try!' The voice boomed out and echoed loudly off the stone walls.

As the figure stepped into the light, Amelia could see that he didn't even appear to be human. He was covered in a black cloak but had no features and his body appeared even darker than his cloak. He moved slowly, like he was gliding, and barely made a sound as he crossed the still courtyard.

'Who are you? You have no business here. We are a peaceful city and want no trouble!' the emperor shouted, having shaken off the original surprise and slowly got back to his feet. He stood proudly on the steps of the temple, determined to show fierce opposition to the threat that his people faced.

'Aahhh, Emperor, how good of you to grace us with your presence. Did eight need to die in order to wake you up though? How disappointing!'

The emperor growled to himself and shouted angrily at his opponent, 'They will be the last of my people to die, trust me. There are far more people here who will defend Orgent against one stranger. You will not last long!'

With this, the stranger laughed, a high-pitched cackle that threatened to deafen all around, and before the emperor's eyes, the figure became two and then four and kept doubling until there were hundreds of the strange dark spectres stood in the courtyard.

'How about now, Emperor? Still feeling confident? How many more opponents do you need?' The stranger pulled open his cloak and what looked like black smoke came pouring out into the courtyard. As the smoke touched the ground, the city was suddenly filled with dark spectres, their numbers dwarfing the population of the city considerably.

The emperor stood speechless, fearing for his life and that of all his people. 'What do you want from us?' The words croaked out of his mouth. He was resigned to defeat and had nowhere left to turn.

'That's a good question, Emperor. We have all the time in the world to talk though, let's give ourselves some privacy.'

The stranger lifted his hand again and twitched his fingers. Suddenly the great doors of Orgent started to creak and groan, slowly closing on their own.

Frightened and without thinking, Amelia ran for the gates. With all the dark smoke still lingering in the air, she was almost invisible in her black cloak. She ran quickly and dived through the gap, just in time to hear the gates loudly crash shut behind her. Lying on the rough ground outside the gates of Orgent, she got to her feet. Her dress was torn and she had cuts on her arms and legs. For the first time in her life she was outside of Orgent. She looked around quickly and saw no one around her. It was just her, the forest and the cliffs. She looked into the distance and could see some light, glowing like a fire. She had no idea where to go, but she knew she had to escape. Looking back at the gates once more, Amelia relied completely on her instinct and started to run.

CHAPTER 14

Amelia thundered through the woodland surrounding Orgent. Her heart was pounding and she could feel every branch that tore at her as she ran for safety. Her dress was ripped to shreds but she didn't dare stop to look at the damage. She knew she had to keep running until the forest cleared and then get as far down the mountain as she could. The night was so dark and the forest eerily quiet around her; the only sounds were the snapping of twigs under her feet and her breathing getting heavier as she covered more ground. Although the forest around Orgent was thick, it wasn't very large, so Amelia made it through quite quickly. She came to a sudden stop after bursting through the last of the woodland and fell to her knees, struggling for breath. Her head was spinning with everything that had taken place and she still had no idea what to do next. At the edge of the forest she could see the steep route down the mountains to the forest and river below, but didn't know what was down there.

In her childhood she had heard tales of the Inuits who lived off of the land below Orgent and had dealings in trade with the emperor and Orgent, but she didn't know whether they were to be feared or not. She couldn't risk being as lost as she was and falling into more trouble. To the east were more mountains and that's where Amelia had seen the glow which she had headed for. She looked again and could still see it flickering gently in the distance. As she knelt on the stony ground looking at the glow, many emotions swept her away at the same time: the thrill of being free; the fear and worry for Orgent and her father; a strange sense of safety that felt almost familiar to her as she watched the glowing light. Her hands and knees were bleeding from all the cuts and she felt exhausted. Beneath the dark night sky, she held her head in her hands and the tears came streaming down her face.

***

Back in Orgent, all the people had been ordered to sit cross-legged with their hands in front of them and their backs against the front doors of their houses. The dark spectres stood watch over them as the main courtyard was left empty. The emperor stood facing his city, waiting for the stranger to speak again. He was carefully scanning the crowd, looking for Amelia; he wanted her by his side where he could keep her as safe as possible but she was nowhere to be seen.

As if reading the emperor's thoughts, the stranger stepped towards him and spoke: 'You are not the only one who wants the princess, Emperor. She is part of my reason for being here and I suggest that she shows herself immediately. If not, I will just have to go through every person here until I find her.'

The emperor roared in response to this challenge. 'You will never get my daughter. I will sacrifice everything before I hand her over to you. Who are you? Why are you here? I demand some answers!'

The stranger laughed at the emperor's show of defiance and began to speak in a slow and menacing tone. 'This story started long ago, Emperor. In the days of old it is written about great powers on earth, sent from our mother herself. As with everything that exists though, there is another way — an adversary, if you like. I am that adversary. I've spent many lifetimes searching for the powers that keep me locked away in my ghostly prison and have never succeeded in defeating them as a whole. This is why I'm here, my dear Emperor. You could say it was your late wife's fault, maybe? How sad that she's not here to face me now, don't you think?'

At the mention of his wife, the emperor exploded in rage and lunged at the evil being with his fists. The city of Orgent watched in shock as he passed right through the figure and landed hard in a heap on the ground behind him.

'Perhaps you should've asked *what* I am rather than *who* I am.'

The evil being laughed loudly, the eerie sound once more reverberating around the walls of Orgent. The emperor slowly got back to his feet, his hands bleeding and his knees aching from where he had hit the ground.

'In the oldest days of our time, the power was trusted to one soul. They were able to perform a great number of acts, which changed life for all those around. It was never a power to be abused though, for with such an act came a great price. As a young man, bestowed with such a gift, I knew better than the elders with their tales of fear and punishments. As I grew stronger, I soon became bored of the prison that their rules put me in, so I did the unthinkable and used the power for my own gain. I would answer to no one and would rule not just that land, but all the lands. I nearly did too, but with being such a young age and having ignored the teachings of the elders, I never knew that the power could be stopped. There were only a few who had learned how to do this, but one wise elder amongst my people managed it. With his act came a sacrifice that he too must suffer through all his lifetimes like me, but his act still leaves him to walk the earth, unlike my ghostly prison. When he performed his ritual, the power was gone; it was split into four separate souls and has remained that way ever since. The body of the boy I was lay dead on the ground, but my soul never settled and I have roamed without life ever since. I have no name, but what I am is the biggest fear that people could ever have. I vowed from that day that I would find the four powers again and become the one. To take back what was rightfully mine and take the Earth as my own, with everything on it having to serve me. This starts tonight, Emperor!'

The emperor had heard fables about powers and wars fought in long ago times, but never believed them to be true. They were just stories to him, back when he was a child.

'What does any of this have to do with Amelia or her mother though? We have no powers here, we are a city of peaceful people who wish for no trouble.'

The stranger moved closer to the emperor, towering over him.

'You are blind to the world around you and you have made your people blind too. Your arrogance tells you that I talk of myth and magic, stories for bedtime and no more. What I speak of is the history of our land and many others. Your wife's history is steeped in the old world order and she was given the responsibility of bearing the world one of those four powers in this lifetime. She had no knowledge of this, and that is how it always must be; it's the only way to keep the powers separate until our mother calls them to join. I followed the power to your wife but had no physical way of getting to her, so I visited her in the night world, determined to find a way to get into Orgent so I could claim that power. However, your wife was stronger than I thought and even managed to fend me off after giving birth. This meant I had to change my plan, and change it is exactly what I did. The connection between your family was so strong that it made Orgent impenetrable, therefore I needed to break that connection. Do you remember the night she died, Emperor? Can you recall what happened?'

The emperor was overcome with sadness as memories flooded his mind. It was a night he'd never forget but chose not to remember.

'We were asleep and I was awoken by the sound of voices. It took me a while to work out what was happening and when I did, I saw Mia opening our window. I called out to her but she kept going, climbing up and out of the window. I jumped out of bed and rushed towards her but it was too late. She seemed to say something to someone and then stepped off the ledge. I always thought she was ill, overcome by some form of madness. You tell me it was you?'

'Yes, Emperor, it was me. I underestimated your wife though. You see, I was trying to get into her head. I needed her to take the princess out of Orgent where I could get to her, but your wife wouldn't break. That evening she chose to die and protect her family. The only good thing that came out of it was your decision to stop people travelling in their dreams.'

The emperor was starting to fight the sadness and get angry. 'How can I have helped you? You got to my wife in her sleep; my medicine stopped you getting to anyone else. I helped none of your plans!'

The stranger laughed to himself, satisfied at all the shocks he was revealing to such an attentive audience. 'Sadly for you, there are two sides to everything, as I said before. Whilst you and your people slept soundly in a dreamless state, I was able to form my plan to get the princess. You are right in stating that it stopped me getting to her, but there are many things you don't know. Let me enlighten you. Those with power can be reached in the land of the sleep but can also see what's heading their way. So you see, Emperor, had you not been drugging all your people then your daughter would've seen my plan and been able to reveal it. So there you are — you are ultimately responsible. How many more have to suffer is up to you. You have two choices. You can hand over the princess and I will be gone, leaving you all in peace, or you can continue to defy me and I promise you, every single person in Orgent will perish until I find her. What is it to be, Emperor?'

The emperor was reeling from taking in everything the stranger had told him. He felt weak but was determined to stand his ground. He couldn't let his people down and he wouldn't lose his daughter. 'These people mean nothing to you — let them go and take me. You could slaughter everyone here and still not find my daughter. Take me and kill me if you choose but I will not hand her over to you — not now, not ever!'

The evil being sighed and glided past the emperor towards the gates of Orgent, addressing the whole of the population. 'People of Orgent, don't be fooled into thinking you will receive quick deaths like the guards did earlier. My powers have many forms and I can cause much suffering. Maybe I should show you what I mean?'

With a swift movement of his arm, he sent one of the last guards flying into the walls of Orgent and kept him pinned against it. The crowd watched as the guard gasped for breath and started to cry out in pain, his face getting redder and redder as the evil being continued his torture from afar.

'What you are seeing is a man consumed from within by the darkest of evils. It feels like fire running through your veins until the body either bursts into flames or just crumbles into ashes before your eyes. This fate will happen to all here until I get the princess.'

'She's gone, I promise you. Please stop, I'll tell you everything!' The guard was howling the words out through the pain surging in his body.

The stranger lowered his arm and the guard dropped to the floor, his skin starting to blister, the pain etched on his face.

'When you closed the doors, I saw her dive through them. The princess is outside Orgent, she was gone before you even spoke of her.'

Still struggling to talk, the guard managed to spit out the last words before slumping in agony on the ground.

'I think we have a problem then, Emperor. This could be a longer night than I suspected.'

'You heard — she's not here, why can't you go? Leave us all in peace, we don't have what you want!'

The emperor's hopes of saving Orgent were fading fast, but at least he knew his daughter was safe.

'That wouldn't work at all. You see, the princess only knows Orgent and will be forced back here eventually. So relax, Emperor. Let us sit and wait for the princess to return.'

***

At the foot of the hills beyond Orgent, Amelia had stopped running. She was exhausted and needed food and rest; she had hardly stopped running since her escape. She reached a large clearing and could see that the glowing light was very close. She was looking through the small patch of trees that sheltered her and could see that the glow was a small fire. The dying embers of the fire had created such a light that she could make out two bodies lying next to it. Amelia knew that the lands surrounding Orgent were full of peaceful natives; there hadn't been any form of war here for a few years now, so she felt safe enough to at least approach them for help. She sat down at the edge of the clearing and quietly watched, looking for any signs of movement amongst the two figures. She didn't want to risk waking them up in case they reacted dangerously to her. Although the natives were mainly peaceful, she thought it wrong for any stranger to surprise them in their sleep and didn't need any more trouble than she already had.

As she sat, she tore off the strips of her dress that were ruined and used them to mop up the blood that was seeping from her many cuts. She didn't realise she had been scratched anywhere but her arms and legs, but in the moonlight there was a small drop of blood on her forehead, in the shape of a tear. Amelia lent back against the tree and before she knew it, she was asleep.

CHAPTER 15

Despite the tiredness that was slowly creeping over his whole body, Majila made giant strides towards the city before him. The weight of Esmee on his back was nothing compared to the emotional weight he felt from all that had brought him here. As he got closer to the city, he slowed down and studied the scene before him. He was a stranger here and had the feeling that he couldn't afford to make any mistakes with whom he trusted or turned to for help. Although there were no walls, the city had different layers of activities, which separated the furthest corners from the temples and buildings which stood in the middle; the closest of these layers to Majila appeared to be a market where many people were bustling around trading a huge range of different things, from food to clothing.

Despite his hunger, Majila knew that the most important thing he had to do was seek someone who might be able to help, house and protect him; he had a small amount of food left in his sack anyway and this could last him longer if needed. From his safe distance, he could see that the locals appeared friendly — no one appeared to be carrying weapons and, though he was a stranger here, he felt confident that he would be received without any problems. As he walked towards the largest group of traders, Esmee tugged on his hair gently and repeated the word he had heard her say before: 'Safe.' It was as if she had read his mind and he felt even calmer in his decision to approach these strangers for help.

There were many people milling around the various stalls and he noticed how much they ranged in age — from the very young children chasing each other around, to the elderly people sitting and creating beautiful clothing from animal furs and other brightly coloured materials. A few people looked his way but they all smiled or nodded as if to welcome him to their home; he wasn't sure whether they were always this friendly or if their interest was softened by the beautiful child he carried steadily on his back. He did his best to smile at as many of the people whose eyes he met whilst carefully searching the area for someone that might be able to help.

After walking through the crowds for some time, he came across an old man who was selling all sorts of herbs and spices at the far end of the market. The man had seen him walking through and had beckoned him over to his stall, showing him all the things he had to sell. After a short discussion, Majila explained to the man that he wasn't looking for anything to buy but that he needed help and he was looking for someone who might be able to protect him and his child. He told the man a little about what had happened at his camp and the man listened intently before leading Majila away from the crowds to a large tent much like the ones they had in his own camp. As he followed the old man into the tent, visions of his people flashed into his mind once more, one minute living happily and the next everything burnt down to the ground. His eyes welled up as he saw Aalym's face again but he knew he had to be strong — Esmee was relying on him to keep going and he wouldn't let her down. The old man moved a seat so that Majila could sit down and then he bowed before heading back out into the open air again. Carefully, Majila slipped the sling from his back and lifted his daughter down onto his lap. She sat right up against him and he protectively put his big arms around her, holding her close while they waited.

As he sat there, he noticed that the tent was even larger than he thought and the part they were in was just half of the area. In it were some papers with some sort of writing on them and some blankets. The only other thing was an empty chair and he wondered what he was waiting for. From behind the curtain separating the two halves of the tent he could smell a strange sweet smoke and when he tried to look to see what the smell was coming from, the curtain moved and a man walked through and stood before him. The man was dressed from head to toe in various animal skins and furs, all woven together and with a string of sharp teeth hung around his neck. In his hand was a metal ball on a chain and the sweet smoke he could smell was spilling out from small holes in the metal object.

'Welcome, I hear you have come to our city seeking help?' the man said in a deep but strangely soothing voice. 'I am a guide for my people here; maybe I can help you too? First I must know that you mean us no harm though, and then you need to tell me your story.' The man sat on the chair opposite Majila, still holding the chain whilst the smoke continued to seep out of the metal ball.

'I can promise you, I am no threat to you or your people. All I seek is safety for my daughter and I. My people are all gone now and we are left without anywhere to go; I fear we may be in danger unless we can get your help. You can search my bag, I have no weapons, just some food for the journey my daughter and I made down from the mountains.' Majila spoke calmly and laid his bag at the feet of this strange man before him.

'That is not necessary — I sense you are a man who can be trusted and what you have in your possession is no business of mine. We are all friends here and if we can help you in any way then we will. My name is Drei Ran, I am known as many things amongst my people — a teacher, a spiritual traveller — but I am the shaman of this land and there are not many problems that I haven't been able to help with in the past. Tell me everything and we shall see what it is best to do for you both.' Despite how frail this old man looked, he had a strength that made Majila believe he would be able to help so, holding Esmee tightly to him, he told the story of what had happened at the campsite, making sure he didn't leave anything out.

As Drei Ran listened carefully to everything that was being said, he sat calmly focusing on the smoke spilling out of his orb, but Majila noticed how he seemed concerned on occasion and how his body appeared to have become more tense as the story unfolded. Exhausted, he finally finished giving Drei Ran all the details and sat back in his chair, rubbing Esmee's back and kissing the top of her head.

'It sounds like you have been through a terrible ordeal, my friend, one I am truly sorry for. However, there is very little either my people or I can do for you, I'm afraid. You see, we live by simple means here, keeping within our region and neither causing trouble or looking for it, so you see we would be unequipped to help you deal with such darkness and violence.' Drei Ran looked uncomfortable as he spoke and Majila couldn't shake off the feeling that there was more to this lack of help than he was revealing.

'You are more than welcome to stay here awhile until you work out your next steps. I'm not sending you away, merely stating that there is no help available to deal with this problem here.'

Majila tried to speak up, but the exhaustion of all he had suffered left him speechless. He fought against the flood of emotions building up in him, determined to appear strong and unshaken, and stood up, hoisting Esmee up onto his back again.

Drei Ran stepped forward and handed a leather bag to Majila, his head bowed and his face stern. 'Here is the only help I can give you, my friend. There are enough coins here to help you pay for somewhere to stay and feed yourself before you head on your way. If you need more while you are here then come and find me. I'm sorry I can do no more. I wish you good luck on your journey.' He dropped the bag into Majila's palm and disappeared back around the curtain from where he had come earlier. Majila was angry and didn't want to stay in the smoke-filled tent anymore, so with Esmee on his back, he headed out into the fresh air again.

With his visitors gone, Drei Ran sat on the ground behind the curtain with his head in his hands, speaking to the sky with his eyes closed. 'Gods above, please let that child leave this city and take these troubles far away. Protect us all from the great powers that threaten and allow us to carry on our existence of peace.' He touched his forehead with both hands and then lay down on the blankets next to him. The sickness washed over him as he thought of these two innocents becoming victims of the dark, but he had the lives of all his people to protect and this was surely the only way.

Majila made his way through the throng of market stalls, built high with wooden frames and all using thin, brightly coloured sheets to keep the traders and goods separated. He felt dejected and couldn't bear to think of what they would do next; his only hope was that he could hide out here with Esmee for a while and hope that Drei Ran changed his mind about helping them before it was too late. He was sure there was something that this strange magic man could do for them, but couldn't push him when he appeared so unwilling to help.

As he walked through the lanes of stalls, Majila became aware of a man in dirty brown robes who appeared to be following him. The man had a big beard and looked like he hadn't washed in a long time, yet he was able to drift in and out of the other people without causing a fuss. Majila stopped at an open doorway of a stall and waited for the man to catch up with him, wondering if he would just walk past without any bother and that maybe all this was in Majila's head as he became more worried about being searched for.

The man ducked past Majila, into the open doorway, and spoke over his shoulder without stopping. 'The magic man couldn't help you, I see? This city is full of cowards. They bury their heads in the sand rather than stand up for what they believe in. Trust me, I have seen it time and time again, it sickened me long ago and it still does today. Follow me, stranger — I have what you need and it would be a pleasure to help you.'

Majila followed the stranger at a safe distance; he didn't know who he could trust and he had the wellbeing of Esmee to worry about. He couldn't fight with a child on his shoulders, yet he didn't dare put her down and risk her being snatched from him. The stranger led Majila through a couple of connected but empty stalls until he reached one that was dark except for an oil-burning lamp in the middle of the room. As Majila's eyes became accustomed to the light, he could see all sorts of weapons laid out on tables. Everything from knives to arrows and other dangerous looking items he had never even seen before were spread out in front of him. The stranger stood between these tables with his arms spread wide.

'Take your time, stranger, and look at all the weapons I have here. Then, when it is time, let the weapon choose you as its owner — you need to feel drawn to it and then you know it is the right one for you.'

'How much are these weapons though? They look costly and I haven't got much to pay with; I still need to buy food and clothes for my daughter.' Majila knew that having a weapon would help protect both of them but couldn't afford not to feed Esmee.

'If something chooses you, it will cost you nothing, stranger. I can see you come from a land where people live differently to us and it's the sort of land I wish I was part of, rather than here where we all hide from anything rather than fight for what we have. It would be an honour to aid you, trust me.'

Majila crouched down and took Esmee from his back, sitting her on the folded-up sling on the floor of the hut.

'Stay,' he whispered, before kissing her cheek and moving over to the tables of weapons. As he stood in front of the tables, he closed his eyes and held his hands out before him, letting them hover over all the different shaped objects before him. It was the sort of thing he had seen his elders do before, around the campfire, and he prayed quietly to himself that they would guide him and this would work. As his hands swept over all the weapons, he found the palm of his right hand become very hot as it stopped in the same area on two occasions. With his eyes shut, he instinctively closed his grip around the object beneath his hand, and lifted it towards his face.

Opening his eyes, Majila looked at what he was holding. In the palm of his hand was the handle of a beautifully shaped sword. It was only about two hand spans long, but it was beautifully formed, with a strong flat edge that joined a sharp curve all the way back to the base of the handle again. On the handle was a curved bit of metal that appeared to serve as some sort of protection for the hand when used in battle. Majila had never seen anything like it and although there were plenty of other bigger swords and bejewelled weapons available, this was his choice. He turned to the stranger and held it out to him.

'The perfect fit for you, stranger — easy to hide but deadly in battle. It chose you well.' The man smiled to Majila and handed him a sheath made from skins that he secured round his waist under his robe.

'Thank you. My name is Majila, so I'm not a stranger anymore.' Majila bowed his head towards the man and slipped the sword into the sheath before concealing it under his clothing.

'Majila, it is my honour. You are all strangers to me though. Come, follow me and I can show you somewhere to sleep.' The stranger passed through a curtain at the back of the stall and motioned for Majila to follow him. Majila picked Esmee up and, as he looked at her smiling face, he felt a faint glimmer of hope for the first time since they had escaped the campsite.

Stepping out through the back of the stranger's tent, Majila found himself entering a white brick building that was attached to the longest tier of the temple. He could just make out the top of the temple, towering over him, the pure white building shining brightly in the sun. The lowest level was a long run of buildings with huge straight steps leading up to the main entrance of the temple and he guessed that this would be the living area for some of those who lived here.

The stranger entered the last of the buildings in the row and waited for Majila and Esmee, before closing the door behind them. Inside were a series of small rooms each with lockable doors made of thick metal bars and sleeping areas made out of blankets heaped together.

'These are our prison quarters, where we keep anyone who breaks the sacred laws of our city. They are rarely used these days but will provide good cover, away from prying eyes. You can stay here with me at night; the doors will be shut but not locked, and during the day you are free to come and go as you please.'

Majila looked around the cramped quarters and sensed that it would be a safe place to hide, but he had one big concern. 'This does seem safe, but what about Esmee? This is no place for a child and she has been through more than enough already.'

The stranger stepped towards Majila and put his hand on his shoulder. 'I have a plan for your daughter but it means being separated from her at night. I know you might fear this, but trust me, I wouldn't have either of you come to any harm.'

'I want to trust you, you have done so much for us already, but I cannot do anything to put Esmee at risk. She is all I have left.' Majila felt troubled, questioning his aide, but he couldn't afford to make any mistakes.

'I understand and I will respect whatever decision you make, but first, please hear me out.'

All three of them sat cross-legged on the floor and the stranger revealed his plan. Along the corridor was the area where the children from the monastery all slept in big comfortable rooms together and Esmee could blend in with them perfectly at night, looking like one of many ordinary children. Then, during the day, she could either join them for the teachings or return to Majila. The children were always guarded and Majila could see her at any time he wished.

Majila looked at Esmee and realised there was a certain safety in her spending time away from him. If whoever destroyed their tribe came for him then she wouldn't be at risk and could escape with others' help. He turned to the stranger and nodded his approval. 'Thank you, we will do what you said and if there is any danger, I can still get Esmee and escape.'

'There is no need to thank me; it is an honour to help you. If we go now, I can show Esmee to the children's quarters and you can both eat, then rest for the night.' The stranger walked over to Majila and offered his hand to help him to his feet.

As the three of them made their way through the bright corridors heading towards the main building, the stranger smiled to himself and spoke over his shoulder to the others. 'My name is Kaliam.'

Later that evening, after settling Esmee, Majila and Kaliam sat and ate together before retiring to their beds to rest. They settled separately in rooms directly opposite each other and as Majila blew out his lamp, he spoke across the hallway. 'Thank you, Kaliam, your help means a great deal to me. We are friends now, not strangers.'

As Majila closed his eyes, he said a quiet prayer to keep Esmee safe and, as visions of the campsite engulfed in flames once more entered his mind, he started to drift off into a troubled sleep.

CHAPTER 16

Black Wolf woke groggily from his sleep. Once again, the vivid dream had asked more questions than it had given answers. There was a dampness in the morning air and as he stretched out to shake the slumber from his limbs, he rolled onto his side and opened his eyes, shocked at what he saw before him.

Crouching close to him was a beautiful woman, wearing a blue dress that had been torn to shreds. She appeared to be covered in cuts on her arms and legs. Quickly, he sat up and reached for his sack whilst scanning the area for any sign of other strangers around.

'I didn't mean to startle you — I mean you no harm. I come from Orgent, my name is Amelia and I need to find help for my people.' Amelia's voice sounded soothing to Black Wolf's foggy head and as he studied her, he could see that she was no threat to him. There was a softness to her that he hadn't seen in any of his people and, as she crouched down near to him, he could feel that she was just as curious as he was.

'My name is Black Wolf. I'm from the tribe that lives in the lowlands, south of these mountains. I have heard of the great walled city before but I know very little about it, I'm afraid. My friend Grey Moon has visited there though and he is wise, so I'm sure he can help you.' Black Wolf smiled at Amelia, speaking as softly as he could so as not to appear at all threatening.

'Thank you, Black Wolf. Although you are a stranger I feel safer already just being here with you.' Amelia felt a strange longing to stay in Black Wolf's company and for a brief moment, here with him, everything did feel better.

As Black Wolf poked at the dying embers of the fire, he noticed that Grey Moon was missing. Nothing else at the campsite had been disturbed though and he knew his friend was more than capable of looking after himself, so he tried not to worry too much. Instead, he carried on poking at the fire until some of the smaller bits of wood caught alight again and tried to avoid staring at Amelia.

'Here, take these blankets. The ground here is very hard; you will get more comfort if you sit on these.' Black

Wolf laid two of his blankets out on top of each other and motioned for Amelia to sit down with him.

'Thank you,' she replied, blushing slightly at his efforts to put her at ease and be so welcoming. She sat focusing on the fire, resisting the urge to stare at him. She had seen drawings of the Inuits in Orgent's historical documents, but never in the flesh. She didn't doubt that his strong features would look fearsome in battle, but she wasn't afraid of him. Instead, she found him strangely attractive and so different to all the other men she had ever known back in Orgent. A part of her deep down inside wanted him to hold her in his strong arms and keep her safe.

These two strangers from different parts of the kingdom sat talking as the fire slowly started to die again. It was only when Amelia asked where Grey Moon was that a familiar voice appeared from the woods nearby.

'I am here, my lady,' said Grey Moon, appearing at the campsite with a sack full of fruit for them all to eat and a couple of small dead animals he had caught for them to cook on the fire.

Amelia and Black Wolf both got to their feet as Grey Moon returned. Amelia held her hand out to him and he took it in his, bowing slightly before her.

'It is a pleasure to finally meet you, my lady. I imagine you have lots to tell me, but first may I ask you to gather some wood for me, then we can eat and you can tell me everything.' Grey Moon smiled warmly at Amelia before tipping the food out onto the blankets by the fire.

'I would be happy to. There are lots of branches near where I slept last night, I shall go and fetch them for you.' Amelia turned and headed towards the woods, enjoying the freedom of having work to do, rather than sitting and watching others do it for her.

After she left, Black Wolf turned to Grey Moon and spoke. 'I thought you had left me, Grey Moon. I wondered where you had gone. I woke up and this stranger was here instead.'

Grey Moon laughed loudly before replying, 'I just went to get food, my child, we will need it with all the travelling we will be doing. It also meant that you both had time to become acquainted.'

'You knew she was here? How long have you known?'

Black Wolf never ceased to be amazed and slightly frustrated by his friend's seemingly infinite wisdom.

'The box prophesised her arrival and when I awoke early I noticed her asleep against the tree over there. I went to get food and I knew that once she woke up, she would have to come over and speak to you. I can't help it if my hunting woke her, can I?' Grey Moon was smiling at Black Wolf and again his friend knew that this wise elder's magic once more played a part here. 'Also, my child, she is many things but certainly not a stranger.'

'Who is she?' Black Wolf was becoming even more curious.

'She has been many things under many different names, my child, and you will soon see this for yourself. Now though, she is the Princess of Orgent, although it appears that to us she just wants to be Amelia.' Grey Moon sat down and started skinning the animals, preparing the food that they would need for the next part of their journey.

Black Wolf stood watching Amelia gather branches in the distance; her beauty transfixed him as he repeated Grey Moon's words quietly to himself, 'The Princess of Orgent.'

Before long, Amelia had returned with an armful of wood and Black Wolf had managed to get the fire roaring again. The morning mist was starting to clear and the heat lifted the damp from their clothes, leaving them feeling warmer again.

Grey Moon had finished preparing the meat and used branches to skewer it and cook it in the campfire during their talk, whilst Black Wolf had used some of their water to soak a pile of rags he'd torn up. He handed these rags to Amelia so she could clean her cuts and freshen up.

'Those cuts look painful, you need to make sure you clean them properly or you may get ill, they are very deep.' Black Wolf couldn't hide his concern — and he couldn't stop watching her, either.

'They do hurt, but I think I've cleaned the worst of them. When I ran through the forest it was so dark and I was going so quickly that the branches kept catching me and slicing me deeply. My legs and arms are fine now but I've still got some on the back of my neck I can feel stinging. Would you mind cleaning them for me? I cannot see them to know if they are clean or not.' Amelia appeared to blush as she handed him a soaking rag and loosened her dress from around her, holding her hair up to reveal her neck to him.

Black Wolf moved closer to her and cautiously dabbed at the scratches on her neck, wringing the dirt and blood out on the floor until they were clean.

'Here, my child, use this to put on the cuts. It's an old remedy our tribe has used since I can remember to help heal battle wounds. Rub it in gently and they should heal well when it dries.' Grey Moon handed Black Wolf a large leaf with a strange light brown paste on it.

Black Wolf appeared nervous at the thought of touching Amelia; this wasn't helped by how beautiful he thought she was, or the fact that he had just found out she was a princess.

'Don't be afraid, Black Wolf, I'm tougher than I look. You can touch me, I won't break.' Amelia seemed to sense his hesitance and he felt she was playing with him.

Black Wolf put some of the paste on his finger and gently traced one of the long cuts that ran down her neck. As his finger touched her soft skin, he felt a strangely familiar spark deep within and suddenly images from his dreams filled his mind.

You are my Aalym, my heart, my lifeblood and I won't leave you. The voice came from within him and he scrambled backwards away from Amelia in shock.

'What was that?' Amelia instantly pulled her dress tightly around her and turned to Black Wolf, her eyes wide in surprise.

'I don't know, I felt something strange and then I heard a familiar voice. I didn't mean to scare you.' Black Wolf struggled to regain his composure as he sat staring at her, his breathing heavy and his mind racing. As he studied her face, he noticed the tear-shaped bloodstain on her forehead and deep in his stomach he felt a sadness that he had never felt before. Without thinking, he moved towards her and gently wiped it from her face, holding her cheek softly in the palm of his hand.

'I'm sorry,' was all he could manage to say and as the tears welled up in his eyes, he turned and walked off from the campsite, into the forest.

Amelia sat there, feelings running through her that she had never felt before either. She placed her hand on her cheek, the warmth of Black Wolf's touch still lingering. 'Black Wolf,' she called out and started to get up to follow him.

'Let him go, Princess, he'll come back when he's ready. He is learning a lot and it will take time to understand it. Don't worry, there is much for us all to discover.' Grey Moon's voice broke the silence and Amelia had forgotten he was sat there.

'What happened, Grey Moon? When he touched me, it felt so familiar but we are strangers. I don't understand any of this, can you explain?' Amelia felt shaken and needed to know what was happening. This world was all new to her and a great contrast to the simple days she had spent in Orgent.

'All in good time, my child, I promise. Events are unfolding as fate wants them to. Do not be scared, we will help each other. It is the Great Mother's way.' Grey Moon looked sympathetically towards her and handed her one of the sticks with meat on it. 'Eat now, Princess, we will need our strength soon.'

After a while, Black Wolf returned to the fire and sat between Amelia and Grey Moon. He took some food and sat quietly eating it, trying to resist the urge to be closer to Amelia. Grey Moon prompted Amelia to tell them what had happened, so she explained in full. She started with the party preparations and didn't stop talking until she had revealed how she'd escaped and the moment Black Wolf had woken up to find her there. 'This is why I need your help. I don't know how much time my father and our people have. They might already be dead, I wouldn't know.' Amelia wept at the thought of what could have happened in her absence.

Black Wolf fought the urge to hold her and keep her safe; instead, he asked about something that had been troubling him from the story. 'You said that this attacker wasn't a person? It appeared as if he was made of thick black smoke. How is this possible?'

'It all happened so fast, but what I saw did look like that. I'd never seen anything like it before, so I took the chance I had and I escaped.' Amelia felt guilty at running, but knew deep down that there was nothing she could have done to stop the attack. She put her head in her hands and broke down again.

'What you speak of is a great evil, my child, and there is a lot of work to be done if we are to stop it. You did the right thing by finding us and we will do everything we can to help your people. Trust me, Princess, and all will be revealed.' Grey Moon put a comforting hand on her shoulder and as she looked up tearfully, her eyes met Black Wolf's through the fire leaving them feeling that unexplainable power again.

'We need to pack up our things now though, we have a long trek ahead of us and shouldn't waste any time.' Grey Moon gathered his belongings, threw his sack over his shoulder, and stood up.

'Where are we going, Grey Moon? Do you know what is happening?' Black Wolf was full of questions as usual as he started to put the fire out.

'I will explain more on the way, but first, we head north.' Grey Moon pointed towards the mountains as Black Wolf got to his feet. 'I will say one thing to you both though and it is very important. Sometimes you can live in each other's hearts for a lifetime and it still takes time for the souls to recognise each other when you meet as strangers.'

Black Wolf moved towards Amelia and held out his hand to help her stand up, and as their palms touched, they almost felt like they knew what Grey Moon meant.

CHAPTER 17

Distracted by the loud fireworks, Elspeth had taken a long time to fetch the emperor's royal drinking vessel. At one point, she had even crouched down under the food preparation table in the kitchen, scared by the noise. When she had eventually gathered everything she needed, she started to walk back to the main entrance so she could give the emperor what he needed and then would be free to continue enjoying the night at Amelia's side.

As she passed a window near the main door, she heard a huge crashing noise and it surprised her so much that she'd almost thrown the serving tray, sending everything flying through the air and hurtling down to the floor, drink seeping out into the cracks of the stone floor. Horrified, she bent down and started to clean the mess up and that's when she heard the loud voice booming out across the city's courtyard.

'Stay on your knees, Orgent, or a far worse fate will come to you. Running or fighting is useless and any who try will perish where they stand.' As Elspeth heard these words, her blood ran cold. Slowly she got back to her feet, crept to the window and looked out, unprepared for the horror she witnessed.

All the people of Orgent gathered in front of their houses, looking terrified. In front of them were dark figures guarding them and Elspeth hadn't seen these people before. Carefully shifting her position, she could make out more guards on the other side of the courtyard. In front of her was a trembling emperor facing an enormous black-cloaked figure. She guessed it had been this huge evil being whose voice she had heard silencing everyone.

Scanning all the faces, she could see no sign of Amelia anywhere; the thought that something might have happened to her filled her with dread. The sense of fear that filled the usually peaceful Orgent was increased by the thick black smoke in the air and the smell of burning flesh.

Elspeth crouched quietly and continued to watch as the horror unfolded before her eyes. She saw the emperor try to attack his enemy, appearing to pass straight through him, collapsing to the ground in pain. Panic rising in her; she knew she had to escape, so she crept carefully back down towards the kitchens.

There was no one inside the palace yet but she thought it wouldn't be long before they came in and took control, so she had to move fast or risk being trapped too. Passing through the kitchen, she made it to the small trade entrance. Although it opened out into the courtyard, she thought it was well enough concealed within the shadows of the palace to provide an escape route. This led to another smaller door in the back wall of the city and would let her out onto the sheer cliff edge behind Orgent. The cliffs here were so steep and ragged that they were practically impossible to navigate through, but it was her only chance of getting away. All the commotion was at the front of the city and the two great doors were already closed.

As she crept along the palace wall, staying carefully hidden within its shadows, she made it to the small door and started to quietly turn the handle. Glancing behind her, she saw a guard burning to death in the distance and knew that it was now or never. She turned the handle fully and the door opened slightly, allowing her enough space, and she started to slip through the gap.

CHAPTER 18

The mountains north of the lowlands were uncharted territory for most of the native people. Only a few had ever ventured into this terrain and most of these visits had happened during the times that war raged amongst the tribes. Over the years, the Inuits had gained enough knowledge that they didn't have to venture far from the lowlands in order to survive, so for Black Wolf this trek would be a step into the unknown.

Although the mountains were steep, there were several small paths that made it easier to reach the higher areas. However, Grey Moon knew that at certain points they would have to climb across some large, rugged parts and this could present many dangers to all of them. He could only hope that they wouldn't need to reach the highest areas, as they were snow-covered all year round and this left that area cold and more treacherous with the ice.

They had been walking for a long time in silence. Grey Moon was leading the way, seemingly concentrating deeply on every step he took, and Amelia followed behind, trying not to show how difficult she was finding the trek. Black Wolf was at the back, constantly scanning the surroundings for any signs of danger and trying to see where they were heading towards.

'Above this next pass there is a small plateau; once we reach it we should stop for food and warmth,' Grey Moon called out to the others.

The path they were following ended abruptly in front of them and instead there were just a few remaining rocks sticking out from the mountains like stepping stones, and on the other side was a small path leading up to a flat sheltered area. Grey Moon hadn't revealed whether he'd been here before but Black Wolf assumed he had, as he seemed to know so much about the mountains and where the plateau was.

Although he was old, Grey Moon moved swiftly even in such treacherous conditions as the face of the mountain, and it was no surprise to Black Wolf when his friend appeared to skip easily across the small steps and make it to the other side, leaving Amelia to try to traverse it next.

'Be careful, child, it's not easy. Just concentrate on your grip and don't look down.' Grey Moon offered Amelia some support as he stood on the ledge waiting for her.

Amelia looked at the steps nervously; all this was such a different world to the one she'd run from in Orgent and she was certain she wouldn't manage much more. Every bone in her body ached and she just longed to be back home in the comfort of the palace instead of risking her life out here on the mountains.

Trying to put all thoughts of the danger out of her mind, she reached across and lifted one foot up onto the first step. As she lifted her other foot, she couldn't help but glance down; the huge drop terrified her. Panicking, she tried to step further but slipped, losing her grip and falling backwards, away from Grey Moon's outstretched hand.

Quickly, Black Wolf leapt to the first step and managed to catch her as she fell, pulling her into him and pinning her against the mountain as the cold winds buffeted his back. The shock had made her feel faint, but Black Wolf's body held her upright.

'Thank you, Black Wolf,' she said breathlessly, her vision meeting his. He stared deep into her eyes and his gaze seemed even more intense than before.

'I won't let any harm come to you, Princess, I promise,' he replied, his lips so close to hers that they were almost touching. Amelia somehow knew that his words were true and as they stood pressed together, she could feel his heartbeat strongly through her chest and again she longed to be held by this enigmatic stranger.

As she recovered her calmness, Black Wolf helped her climb across the steps until she was able to reach Grey Moon's hand and step to safety. Before long all three had made it safely to the other side and were ready to continue their trek.

They walked up the small path and Grey Moon was right; they found themselves on a small plateau, well-sheltered from the wind and with a shallow cave for extra cover.

'You need to rest for a while, Princess. We should all eat to help us keep up our strength, and I need to light a fire.' Grey Moon was rummaging around in his sack, pulling out some food for all of them and all other manner of strange powders and pastes.

Amelia laid out the blankets she'd had tied round her, so they could sit down, whilst Black Wolf separated the food up so they each had some. Grey Moon was gathering bits of dry leaf and sticks, building a small fire in the entrance to the cave.

'I don't think we'll get much heat from that,' Black Wolf said as he watched his friend light the tiny fire.

Grey Moon laughed loudly and it echoed round the cave before he responded. 'No, my child, you have it all wrong. This is not for heat, this is for directions.' And he sat down mixing powders before throwing them into the fire.

'Directions? I don't understand...' As he spoke, Black Wolf's sentence was cut short by the patterns that seemed to appear out of the fire before him.

Where the flame lapped towards the sky, he saw the figure of a wolf emerge, heading straight up before disappearing into the smoke, then what looked like a figure sat round a small fire appeared before him and then vanished.

'How are these directions though, Grey Moon? We need more than visions,' said Black Wolf.

'My child, sometimes all you need is an open heart and mind,' Grey Moon replied, before their conversation was disturbed by a piercing wolf howl coming from behind them.

Black Wolf turned quickly and at the end of the plateau was a beautiful but ghostly looking wolf, sitting still and facing directly up the mountains, as if he was waiting for them to follow him. Black Wolf moved to follow, but Grey Moon caught his arm, stopping him.

'We have time, Black Wolf. We need to eat and make sure the princess has recovered enough to continue — it was quite a shock she had on the mountain. I don't think we have much farther to go now, our guide will wait for us.'

'It all seems to be about waiting though and I don't understand what's happening. I cannot even touch Amelia without feeling sad and my head showing me all sorts of strange visions. I need to know more.' Black Wolf was starting to become impatient and could no longer hold his frustration in.

'I promise you it will all make sense soon enough, my child. You have come a long way on your own personal journey and I will tell you more once we get to our next destination. Do not fear the feelings or visions, open your heart to them and you will answer your own questions.' Then, changing the subject instantly, he turned to Black Wolf and said, 'Let us eat now. We need to start moving again before too long.'

Grey Moon guided Black Wolf over to where Amelia was sitting and although he knew he would have to reveal more soon, he knew that now was not the time.

The three of them ate quickly, sitting in their own little worlds, and hardly a word was spoken. Eventually, their silence was broken by another loud wolf howl and Grey Moon smiled to himself as if he was expecting it all along. Having finished his food, he reached into Black Wolf's sack and removed the box, placing it in front of them.

They all looked at the box and saw both symbols that were already lit up, now joined by a third glowing symbol. The symbol was fiery red and shaped like a flame, and before Amelia or Black Wolf could say anything, Grey Moon got to his feet and spoke, 'We must go now, we are very close.'

Once again, Black Wolf and Amelia both followed him, heading on the next part of their strange journey. The only difference was that this time they were following a ghostly looking wolf who led the way further up the mountains.

CHAPTER 19

Lone Wolf sat quietly in his cave, awaiting the visitors that his fire meditations had shown him. The ghostly wolf had disappeared and not returned but he was sure that it wouldn't be very long before it came back again, and he had the feeling that once it did, his life would never be the same again.

As he sat staring into his fire, he thought about his life high up in the mountains and how long it had been since he'd had the company of others. Although it had been years, he could remember his time amongst his tribe as if it was yesterday, but whenever his mind turned to those days, the heavy feelings of loss returned.

In those days, there were many small tribes living separately throughout the land and they were always at war with each other, all desperately trying to be the one major force that could rule the area. Despite being one of his tribe's youngest members, he had learnt the ancient arts and customs quickly, rising to be a prominent figure amongst his people, especially in battle, and he was a natural at it.

Gazing into the flames, he saw the familiar faces of his mother and father appear. He thought of them often, full of regret, wishing he could talk to them again. He remembered the day he had lost them so vividly that every time he thought of it, he had to deal with all the raw emotions again. He recalled that morning with ease, as he'd said goodbye to his parents and led his tribe out on a hunt, desperate to secure both food and safety for his people. After a long day's hunting, his tribe had returned home to find their camp totally destroyed. It appeared as if something had blown through the area, devouring everything in its path and then disappeared without a trace. Without any thought of their own safety, all the returning tribesmen had rushed straight to what was left of their homes and found bodies littering the area. Lone Wolf had run straight to his hut and found the charred bodies of his parents lying next to each other by their fire. A series of emotions had quickly risen up inside him, starting with fear, then shock, before a painful anger caused him to roar towards the sky, with tears flowing down his face. Ignoring the others, he had carried their bodies deep into the forest and laid them to rest in an opening by the stream where they had always loved to walk together. He had said his goodbyes to them and left nature to slowly cover them as their religion wished, hoping they could find peace at last in such violent times. Once he had finished his sad goodbye, he had slowly walked away from the tribe and all the fighting, never once stopping to look back.

It had taken time for Lone Wolf to get used to living alone, but eventually he had found a peace that he'd never felt before and his self-imposed isolation had served him well. He still used his old teachings to keep up with the tribe's customs but hadn't felt the need to surround himself with others again. The art he indulged in most was fire meditation, and through it he had learnt a lot about himself and what was happening in the land around him. The time of war had long since gone and the tribes had all finally found peace as one, but still the scars of his parents' death went unhealed and he vowed one day he would discover the truth and take revenge. As the sky above him began to darken, Lone Wolf loaded more wood onto the fire and watched the flames rise high into the sky. In the distance, he heard a howl, and he waited.

Farther down the mountain, the group continued to follow the ghostly wolf. It was starting to get dark and Black Wolf was worried that they might end up stranded on the mountain before they reached their destination, but Grey Moon continued to trek with determination.

Not wanting to involve Amelia, Black Wolf caught up with Grey Moon and spoke quietly to him as they walked. 'You know I'd follow you anywhere, Grey Moon, but I'm going to need answers soon. I need to understand all these dreams and the feelings I've been having, I'm struggling to keep going with all this dragging me down.'

Grey Moon could see how heavy this all weighed on Black Wolf's shoulders and wanted to help, but knew that the time wasn't quite right. 'You need to trust me, child. I promise you I will reveal everything as soon as I can, but this is bigger than just you or me. We haven't got far to go now and then I will tell you everything I can.'

As Grey Moon carried on walking, Black Wolf waited for Amelia to catch up. He didn't understand his need to be close to her but he knew in his heart that this must all mean something and he trusted Grey Moon enough to know eventually it would all make sense.

'Grey Moon said it's not much farther, Amelia, and then we can rest.' He held his hand out for her, helping her climb the path so she was standing level with him and as their hands touched they both felt the strange energy again.

'Thank you,' was all she said as she stood facing him, their eyes burning deeply into each other's.

Black Wolf moved closer to her, brushing twigs out of her hair, letting his hand linger longer than was necessary. There was so much he wanted to say to her. Unbeknownst to him, Amelia felt the same. She held his hand against her face, tracing his rough fingers gently with hers and slowly leant towards him until they were almost kissing.

'Amelia,' Black Wolf said breathlessly, and he leant in closer until a voice broke the tense silence between them.

'We are here, I can see the fire,' Grey Moon called out over his shoulder and it provided enough of a distraction to break them apart quickly and follow the sound of his voice. As they climbed the last part of the path, there was another loud wolf howl, the piercing cry mirroring the strange longing in their hearts.

The ghostly wolf reappeared from over the closest rise to Lone Wolf's cave and ran into the fire, disappearing without a trace in front of him. He got to his feet and walked forward, watching as an elderly native appeared before him, closely followed by a younger, stronger looking native, and finally a beautiful looking woman who wore a torn dress but still looked like no one he had ever seen before. The three strangers stood together facing him, the roaring fire between them reflecting in their eyes as the flames continued to leap towards the sky.

'Greetings, I've been expecting you,' said Lone Wolf, not moving from his spot.

'Greetings to you, my friend. I am Grey Moon and this is Black Wolf, we are from the tribe that lives in the lowlands, and this is Amelia, she is from Orgent.'

Grey Moon bowed to Lone Wolf and held out some food as an offering to their host. 'I know who you are, Grey Moon, it is an honour to meet you. I am Lone Wolf. If you are here with the princess from the great walled city then I imagine this is even more important than I thought? Please, come sit, I think we have lots to discuss.' Lone Wolf motioned for them to sit round the fire and the travellers couldn't wait to rest and finally learn more about these extraordinary happenings.

The group had been talking for a while as they ate. The fire was still roaring as they had discussed their journey up the mountain and where they had come from. Grey Moon had made Amelia describe events at Orgent, and when she had finished they all sat in ominous silence, each with their own thoughts and questions that needed answering. Eventually it was Grey Moon who broke the silence by addressing the group.

'I'm sure you all have many questions for me and I'm not surprised. I will answer everything and tell you what you want to know, but first I need to tell you what is happening in Orgent, and that's a story with deep roots in the history of our land.' Grey Moon made himself more comfortable and spoke slowly.

'In an age where our world was created, the Great Mother bore a child that shared her immense powers. She hoped that these powers would be used for good and left her child to find his own way, but sadly human emotions proved a stronger temptation for he who held these powers than she had expected. It wasn't long before he became tired of not being allowed to use these powers and then somewhere far back in time, one of the purest hearts turned dark and started dabbling with ancient magic in order to control the lands. This lack of knowledge and ability to control these powers unleashed an even darker force within him, which he lost control of, and this bad feeling seeped into our people, causing all our tribes to start fighting with each other. Many people have fought this evil before but only those who hold the original Mother's powers in them can banish it. Every time the evil is banished, people think it has gone for good, but all it ever does is lie in wait for another chance to strengthen and then attack again. This is the dark force that has taken control of the great walled city, Princess. These are dark times for us all and it is up to us to save your people.' Grey Moon stopped talking and took a drink, knowing there would be lots of questions.

Amelia was the first to leap in and talk. 'Why attack Orgent though? My people are peaceful and never looked for trouble anywhere. What can we do to save them?'

'There are four parts to our Great Mother's power, Princess, and these parts have been separated over the years by the magic of the elders, at our Great Mother's wishes. If one person held the power and was defeated, then we would forever be in darkness, but this way there are four separate chances for the good souls to defeat the evil, and if any of these good souls are killed, then their power comes back in the next life. This is why the evil has to hide and wait; once it can gather all the good souls together then it has a chance to defeat it for good and rule over us all. It has traced one of the four to Orgent and it knows the others will join there to try to defeat it. It never allowed for that one to escape before it closed its walls though.' Grey Moon looked at Amelia and his eyes said everything she needed to know.

'Surely you don't mean me? I've never even ventured outside the walls of Orgent until now. There's nothing special about me, I promise you.' Amelia struggled to understand what Grey Moon meant.

'You haven't left Orgent in this life, Princess, but in your past you were as native as the rest of us. Your father tried to protect you and your people by stopping journeys to the night world, but sadly this has caused more harm than good. I will show you, if you wish?'

Amelia looked at Black Wolf sat quietly next to her. There was something about him and the fire nearby that was affecting her deeply but she didn't know why. 'What's my father got to do with this?'

'If you had been able to dream, you would have seen what was coming for you, Princess, and learned more of your own history. The medicine made it hard for the power to get to you but also stopped you being prepared for its arrival.' Grey Moon spoke solemnly; it was hard for him to reveal things to such an innocent as Amelia, but she needed to know the truth.

'I remember dreaming the night I escaped, wild dreams full of fire and sadness. I didn't realise then, but I do now, that I cannot remember dreaming before then. Please, show me what you can.'

Grey Moon had started mixing some herbs from his bag whilst they'd been speaking and had made some into a sticky paste. With his finger, he drew a line down her forehead and sprinkled some drier herbs into the fire, awaiting the magic.

Suddenly, everything but the fire seemed to disappear from Amelia's view, replaced instead by a vast camp of tents in a forest opening. There was a beautiful green-eyed child sat on her lap, playing with her hair. She was smiling and the happiness she radiated was infectious. Looking up from her lap into the distance, she saw a muscular tribesman with long hair walking towards them. He sat down with them and the girl immediately held out her arms for him to hold her. 'My beautiful Esmee, I've missed you,' he said, before turning towards her and putting his hand gently on her cheek. 'Aalym, you are certainly a sight for sore eyes. I hope our little one hasn't been causing you too much trouble?' He smiled at her and kissed her passionately on the lips.

'No more trouble than her father is,' she replied. 'I've missed you, Majila, and longed to feel you close.' She kissed him again and then everything turned a beautiful bright white.

Immediately, the scene was very different. There was fire everywhere and as a strange black ash flooded through her tent, she was left on the floor, bloodied and broken, desperately trying to hold on to the life she could feel slipping from her grasp. Feeling something grab at her dress, she looked down to see Esmee, blackened by the smoke, crying and holding onto her. Then Majila came bursting in to save them. Everything flashed by so quickly — their last goodbye, the kiss and parting words, the two of them escaping — then nothing but darkness.

Amelia sat bolt upright around the fire, unaware she'd even been lying down, struggling to cope with what she'd seen. Tears were streaming down her face and when she said one word — 'Esmee' — her hand immediately held her stomach.

Black Wolf stared at her in shock. 'What did you just say?' he asked as he moved closer to her, holding his hand out to touch her.

'My Esmee,' she repeated, automatically reaching for his hand and holding it tightly, instantly transferring everything she'd seen directly to him. This time he didn't leap back in shock; instead he pulled her towards him tightly, holding her close and letting her release all her sadness.

Grey Moon looked at Lone Wolf. He was sat there looking both confused by what was happening and concerned for the princess, who appeared crushed by what she had seen.

'I wish that was all, but there is more for all of you,' he said before sitting quietly again.

CHAPTER 20

Elspeth was trembling as she slipped through the door in the back wall of Orgent. In all her time living here, she had never known it be used and was unsure of how she'd manage to get much farther without plummeting to her death. She had to try though because she was sure the other option would be worse.

Stepping out onto the ledge, she could feel a cold wind blowing around the side of the mountain and realised this would make it even more difficult to manoeuvre around. Her best chance was to step sideways along the ledge, clutching any parts of Orgent's wall that protruded, and try to make it onto the edge of the city, and flatter land. Tentatively, she started to turn to face Orgent and slip out onto the ledge as the door started to creak shut behind her. Just as she searched for a foothold, the door swung wide open again, splintering against the inside wall before a massive cloud of black ash tore Elspeth from the wall. She screamed as she was swung out in a wide arc, over the mountains below. She was then pulled back through the doorway she'd just escaped from by her feet. Inside the walls again, she felt herself get dragged along the floor, every rock scraping against her as her body was roughly thrown about, finally ending up at the feet of the stranger.

'You dare to think you could escape? Me, with all the power I wield, against you, a mere serving girl.' The stranger's voice was angry and loud, causing Elspeth to curl up, cowering. 'Stand up and face me, girl, or I will make you suffer even more than I have already.'

Elspeth crawled backwards slightly towards the emperor, desperately trying to get any protection she could. The emperor looked beaten and drained of all hope as he looked at her solemnly and spoke with his head bowed, 'Just do it child, we cannot fight, we must do as he says.'

Slowly, Elspeth got to her feet. She was bruised and bloodied from being dragged along the courtyard but nothing was broken so she was able to stand. 'W-what do you want from me? As you said, I'm just a servant girl

— I'm of no use to you.' She stammered as she spoke, looking up at this huge, menacing figure.

'I know who you are and I know how close the princess is to you, so trust me, you will be useful to me. You and this fool's privileged daughter share a bond, so you will help me get her back here.'

'Never, I will never help you. There is nothing you can do to me that would make me help you or betray the princess.' Fighting the urge to run, Elspeth hissed her words at him in an act of defiance.

As he moved closer towards her, the evil being's featureless face changed slightly and two piercing red eyes appeared amongst all the black.

'There is much I can do to you, girl, and I will. I am born of the fire which all of mankind denies it has in itself — the fires of greed, hatred and the blackest of hearts. You will help me or I will make you as I am, just for my own amusement.' As he spoke, he raised his hand to her and twisted it in mid-air, causing her neck to snap back at an awkward angle.

The emperor shouted, 'Please, stop —!'

'Silence!' the stranger screamed at him, and used his other hand to send the emperor flying backwards onto the floor again. 'Now, I will ask you again — and think carefully before you answer. Will you help me or not?' His red eyes were burning like fire as he spoke to her.

'Never,' was all she managed to say breathlessly, the angle of her head causing her immense pain.

'Then I shall have to find other uses for you,' he replied, letting her head drop forward again before sending her crashing against the city walls.

The city watched as a cloud of black ash left his body and hovered around Elspeth, pinned against the wall by the evil being's power, before slowly tearing her dress open at the neck. She was powerless to stop anything as the ash seemed to disappear down inside the material, leaving her hanging there, crying.

'Please just let her go, she is little more than a child,' the dazed emperor pleaded. He avoided looking at his Elspeth's body being cruelly revealed to everyone, seemingly just to humiliate her.

'A child to you maybe, Emperor, but to me she is a

woman and little more than an amusing way to fill the time until she changes her mind and chooses to help me — or I will end her.' The evil being's dark laugh echoed once more around Orgent's cold stone walls.

Elspeth started to weep loudly and it seemed her dress was slowly being torn open more, displaying her flesh for all to see. She couldn't move at all and every part of her body felt like it had a huge weight pressed against it. All she could do was close her eyes and hope it would be over soon.

'You are very beautiful for a servant girl... Maybe I should make you my queen when I take this throne and rule the lands. What do you think, Emperor?'

The emperor turned away, tears in his eyes, but the evil being used his power to put the emperor on his knees, facing Elspeth's semi-naked figure, unable to move or look away.

'Just kill us — there is no need to defile this girl. She is innocent,' he begged.

'Kill you all, Emperor? Where would the fun be in that? Besides, I have a lot more for you to watch yet, the night is young.' He laughed, his eyes flickering an even deeper shade of red.

As Elspeth hung there, her body on display like meat in the city's market, she felt the night get even colder and feared what would come next.

CHAPTER 21

Back in the mountains, Black Wolf and the princess were still sat holding each other tightly. She was slowly calming down but they were both silent, leaving Lone Wolf to speak to Grey Moon.

'So what is my role in all this, Grey Moon? I've lived up here for so many years now and haven't met any of you before, are you just here for my help?' Having heard Grey Moon's explanation of the link between the other two, he failed to understand his part in what was happening.

'You are just as important, Lone Wolf, and the evil has taken from you not just in your last life but in this one too. The dark force, the ash, the destruction, you remember it all too well.' Grey Moon spoke gently, desperate not to provoke an angry reaction, but he needed Lone Wolf to see it for himself.

'My parents?' he replied, his fists balled tightly in anger.

'Yes, but please allow me to show you the rest.' Grey Moon painted more of his paste on Lone Wolf's head and once more threw herbs into the fire.

Lone Wolf was used to the customs of the tribes and lay down on the ground, closing his eyes and waiting for the visions to start. Before long he was transported to a busy market stall at the base of a huge white temple. He watched as a tribesman came seeking help with a beautiful child strapped to his back. Where no one was prepared to help, he would. He took them to safety after supplying the native with a weapon.

As quickly as the vision appeared, it was gone again, and Lone Wolf sat upright once more, turning to Grey Moon.

'I didn't see much, just enough to recognise Black Wolf and a child. Is this the same child that the princess saw? What did I do for them?' He had even more questions now than he did before the vision.

'Yes it is, you were known then as Kaliam. A true believer in good and helping those who needed it. You were a warrior and a defender of others, as you have been throughout your many lives. There is more to see, but that will come to you over time, these things should not be rushed.'

On hearing the name Kaliam, Black Wolf let go of

Amelia slowly and looked up at Lone Wolf. 'It's you — you helped me when no one else would?' He got to his feet, trying to shake all these thoughts out of his head, desperate for some clarity and understanding.

'You have all seen parts now and there will be more, but it must happen in its own time. Three of the chosen four are here now and once we find the fourth, we can all move forward together, end this evil and save Orgent.'

'What about you, Grey Moon? You are not one of the four?' Black Wolf said, surprised that his magical friend was not a power.

'I am the great elder who the spirit of our Great Mother turned to when she needed the wrong undoing. I was one of a few who could perform the magic needed to take the power back and split it into four souls. In doing this, the child was taken and forever trapped in the ghostly prison he has inhabited ever since. I sacrificed a normal life and many other things to do this. I walk through each life as an elder, never again to experience the joys of youth, and unable to have a family of my own as it would be too dangerous for them. The Great Mother only allowed for the four powers to be reunited when the time was right, in order to defeat the evil, and that time is now.' Grey Moon was starting to tire now and was hoping he would soon be able to rest.

'What about my people though? This is all taking so much time; surely we will be too late?' Amelia's thoughts had suddenly snapped back to the present and the trouble at Orgent.

'Time has stopped in Orgent, Princess. The evil can only appear for a short time otherwise its power lessens quickly. Its only chance is to stop time and wait for us to fight it, then if it wins it has full power, always, and can reign over this land and all others. At Orgent, it is the same night you left, and it will stay frozen in time and darkness until the evil wins or you can defeat it. We still need to move quickly though as its power grows with every life it takes, and if we don't go there soon, there might be no one left to save.' As Grey Moon finished speaking, the group was interrupted by the piercingly familiar howl of a wolf, and once more the ghostly animal appeared before them, walking over to the mouth of the cave and lying down.

'This wolf has appeared regularly before your arrival,

Grey Moon, what does it mean?' Lone Wolf asked the question he'd wanted answering for days.

'The wolf has been held in the highest regard amongst our tribes since the earliest of days. The magic of its soul is still not fully known, but it is the one animal we have never hunted; instead, we have shared its land and respected its power like it does ours. The few skins we have taken have always been from wolves that were already dead and we always offered a sacrificial prayer as a thank you for these. The wolf you see now is our spirit guide, here to represent the threat this evil poses to us, and if we follow it, it will lead us where we need to be. Tomorrow it will take us to the Charmed Forest, where we will meet the fourth soul, and then we will be complete. Tonight we must rest though. I know there is more to learn but I am tired, so will bid you all goodnight.' Grey Moon slowly got to his feet, taking the blanket, and settled down in the cave, leaving the others by the fire.

Left sitting in silence, Lone Wolf turned to the others and spoke quietly and quickly. 'We still have lots to talk about, but I think I will turn in now too. I have many things to ponder... Goodnight.'

Black Wolf and Amelia said goodnight and sat together awkwardly by the fire. He turned to her and said, 'I cannot say that I understand any of this, Princess, but I know how I feel and I know this isn't the first time we've met. There's so much I want to say but I don't know how.' He lifted his hand, cupping her face towards him and as their eyes met, the passion between them could not be denied.

'I know, Black Wolf, there is nothing we need to say tonight though, so let us just sleep. Can I sleep here next to you? I'd feel safer if I could.' She covered his hands with hers as she spoke.

'Yes, Princess, whatever you wish. I'm staying up for a while, but I will be here to protect you, I promise.' Then he leant in and kissed her on the cheek before she lay down next to him.

Black Wolf gathered his sack and took out the book that Grey Moon had given him, already filled with thoughts and dreams. He carried on writing in it, desperate to make sure that he left nothing out. As his mind started to turn to the face of Esmee, he heard a sleepy Amelia mumbling next to him.

'I'm not a princess, I'm Aalym, your love,' she said sleepily, before drifting off into the night world.

Black Wolf smiled sadly to himself and then carried on writing in his journal. As the flames crackled beside him, he looked at her and felt complete for the first time ever.

CHAPTER 22

The flaming arrow flew through the dark night sky, plunging deep into the elder's chest. He cried out in agony as the flames caught his furs alight, setting him on fire in an instant. In desperation, he stumbled forward, falling to the ground, and crawled back to his hut for help. As he crawled, he saw arrows flying into the camp from all directions, the fires spreading throughout the huts and destroying everything in their path. He reached his hut just as a swarm of dark-cloaked figures descended into the camp, grabbing other members of his tribe and throwing them out into the open. Through his pain, he watched as throats were slit and bloodied bodies were dumped to the ground, in a pile before him. As he felt his skin burning, the pain became too great and he slumped forward, unable to move another muscle. As the life ebbed painfully from his burning body, he heard a familiar voice coming from somewhere close. This voice was barely a whisper yet it spoke words that brought him some comfort in his final moments.

'Take these souls lightly, dear Mother, and let the light of the moon grant them a chance again, with nothing but goodness in their hearts. Let them begin a new journey.'

The fire returned, a blanket of flame was all there was. He didn't feel afraid though; he knew this was his destiny. To walk through the fire would mean that everything would be revealed to him. The Great Mother's tears would cool his fevered skin, if only he would walk into the flames.

Beyond the flame was a clearing in dense woodland. There was a strange thick mist in the air, but he could just make out a shape in the centre which looked like a figure. He made his way through the mist and arrived at what turned out to be a tree stump, covered in claw marks. As he stepped closer he heard a baby cry and when he looked into the stump, he realised it had been hollowed out and lying in the middle was a baby wrapped in furs, alone and crying in the middle of the forest. As he put his hands on the stump, he noticed the two pawprints, pressed into the bark. They were so deep they looked almost like they were carved into the wood. Somewhere in the distance, he heard the loud howl of a wolf and then the mist blinded him completely.

He felt hands lifting him up, removing him from his small, safe place. A stranger's face appeared, kind and gentle, leaning over him. Behind this man was a beautiful clear night sky, all the stars were shining and they were overshadowed by just one thing: a full, grey moon.

CHAPTER 23

To the west of the lowlands, far below Orgent, there was a part of the forest that the natives had never seen before but had often heard tales of as children. They were known as the 'Charmed Woods', and stories were told around campfires of all manner of strange creatures who lived there. The truth was that no one knew what was there, as they had never been there before. The tales scared some children and amazed others, but most didn't believe the woods existed at all.

This mystical place really did exist though and was inhabited by four of the land's strangest dwellers. They were a group of four faery folk, all female and living peacefully together, as had the other faery folk before them. Although to them the woods always existed in the same place, such was the power of their charm and magic, that they could keep it hidden from the view of others, so much so that only the strongest of magic men could ever locate it.

The river that ran along the base of the mountains culminated in these woods, in a beautiful lake, and standing over the lake was an ancient tree of which the faeries have their own campfire stories to tell. The woods had been a source of great magic since the beginning of time and the faeries never dared share their secrets with others; this is what led to them living in seclusion, generation after generation, happily hiding away from all the troubles that others cause.

As the land around them became involved in a fight against evil, the four faeries were all enjoying a quiet day by the lake.

Ember's voice interrupted the chatter of the others. She was the wisest of the group and she was a devoted student of the natural arts that faeries had taken part in since time began.

'Something is coming our way, sisters. I've felt it in the air the last couple of nights. I think we might be having visitors soon.'

'What do you mean "visitors"? We can't have visitors, you know that, Ember.' Luna looked up from her food preparation, dismissing her friend's warning. Luna was the head of the faeries, mainly due to her even temper and ability to stay level-headed in almost any situation.

'Something has happened out there, I don't know what, but I think it's bad. It's just a feeling I get, and anyway, we can have visitors. They just need to know where to look.' Ember didn't want to argue, but she knew she was right.

'We should ask the Great Mother then; she'll provide us with an answer.' Luna knew she could only calm any of their fears by using the customs to seek an answer.

'Ask her for some handsome faery boys too,' came a shout from Aira, as she came rushing out of the woods, knocking Luna's food everywhere. Aira was the youngest of them all, naïve, playful and accident prone, which was a bad combination at times for all of the others, who were constantly clearing up her mess.

'We need to group together if we are to ask the Great Mother — where is Tallulah?' Ember tried to get everyone's attention whilst Luna picked up her food, muttering to herself.

Tallulah was the most inquisitive of the four, always asking questions and seeking answers. She was the most solitary of the group and could often be found sitting alone somewhere, trying to find her place in the world.

'I'm here,' she said, quietly wandering out of the woods towards the others. 'What's all the fuss about?'

'Ember senses something is wrong in the world around us and thinks we might have visitors soon. So we need to perform an element ritual and see what our Mother tells us.'

Luna took charge of the situation and gathered everything they needed to perform their ancient faery custom.

First, Luna drew a faery circle in the ground, with mounds of earth to frame the area, before placing dry leaves and twigs within the circle. Then Ember rubbed two stones together, creating a spark that lit the fire they needed, setting the leaves alight as the sound of crackling filled the air. Next, Aira used a faery reed pipe to blow into the fire, causing the flames to grow and spread higher, before finally Tallulah filled a clay bowl from the lake and sat it in the middle of the fire.

As the other three faeries sat round the fire, chanting in an ancient faery language, Ember closed her eyes and spoke.

'Our dear, Great Mother, we offer you from all the elements and ask for your guidance. Please reveal the truth behind our fears and give us the courage to face what lies ahead. We, your children of nature, bless you and offer our love as a way of thanks.' Then they all sat quietly and waited, staring at the steam slowly rising from the bowl of water.

As they watched, the steam thickened and a vision appeared to them. It showed a beautiful, lush green forest, consumed by a black cloud that left nothing but burnt skeletal remains of gnarled branches and ashen tree stumps. Then the steam revealed four figures walking through the forest, healing the broken nature around them, and then the last vision showed a huge white building falling apart until all that remained was rubble. Eventually the steam cleared and the faeries sat together deep in thought.

'You were right,' Luna said to Ember, frowning with concern.

'What are we going to do? Those visions looked terrible — the forest was destroyed. What does it all mean?' As usual, Tallulah was affected most by what they had all seen. She wanted answers.

Ember looked up solemnly from the fire and spoke quietly to them. 'I think we'll find out soon.'

CHAPTER 24

Black Wolf sat upright, shaken by his dream. Amelia was lying next to him and, stirred by his movement, she rolled over and looked at him.

'What's wrong, Black Wolf?' she asked as she put her hand on his back to try to calm him.

'It's just the fire again, Princess, and visions from my childhood. I'm okay, but I need to speak to Grey Moon immediately.' He took her hand and gently removed it from his damp skin before getting up and walking towards the cave.

In the mouth of the cave, Lone Wolf was packing belongings into a sack and Grey Moon was sat quietly, apparently deep in thought.

'Good morning, Black Wolf,' he said without looking up. 'Let's go for a walk, shall we?'

Together, the two of them walked away from the camp and sat side by side looking out over the mountains.

'What troubles you, my child?'

'I had a series of visions, Grey Moon. They were all short flashes but I need to make sense of them. Can I talk to you about them?' Black Wolf was dazed by the vividness of what he'd seen and hoped his friend could help shed some light on what they meant.

'I will do my best to help you, my child; however, this is your journey, so I'm not sure how much help I can be.'

'I saw the same scene as before but from a different view. I remember saying a prayer to one of the fallen elders in my first vision back at the lowlands, but this time I heard myself saying it to someone nearby. Then I walked through a great fire and I was in the woods where you took me when we set out on our journey.' Black Wolf stopped to take a breath as his friend shifted uncomfortably next to him.

'What did you see in the woods, my child?' Grey Moon asked.

'I saw the tree stump and heard a baby crying. The baby was inside, wrapped in furs, and the stump had pawprints on it, possibly left by wolves. Then I was looking up and a stranger lifted me; all I remember seeing was the beautiful full moon behind him though. I know it was me as a child, but who was the stranger and what does it all mean?' Black Wolf felt like the answer was just out of his grasp.

'I don't know what to say, my child. You must follow your own instinct and all will become clear. That part of the journey is very personal to you; stay calm and focused, and you will learn more. We need to get moving soon though. We have a long journey ahead.' Grey Moon got up quickly and moved away without any eye contact, leaving Black Wolf even more confused. He didn't want to join the group until his mind was calmer, so he decided to sit alone with the wind whistling around him on the mountainside.

'Here you are, stranger. I was worried about you.' Amelia's voice roused Black Wolf from his daydream after he'd been sat there a little while.

'Sorry, Princess. I just needed time to sit and think after my talk with Grey Moon. I've been trying to make sense of all this madness.'

'Did he help you?' Amelia asked, sitting down closely next to him.

'He said he couldn't, but I feel like he's keeping something from me. I'm just so confused. I feel like I'm caught between a world I barely remember and the world we're in now.' Black Wolf looked tearful and hung his head low.

'I cannot imagine how hard it must be for you, but I know how you feel with the confusion. I'm supposed to be the princess of Orgent, but when I'm with you I feel like Aalym. I can't explain it but there are so many feelings for me to deal with.' Amelia put her arm around Black Wolf, holding him close to her.

'It must be hard for you too, Princess, coming from a sheltered life in the great walled city and thrown out into the wild with all the worry of what might be happening to your people. I wish there was something more I could do for you. I feel lost most of the time, apart from when you are close.' He looked up at her and she could feel the passion burning deep within him. She pulled him even closer and they sat silently with so much left unsaid between them.

At the cave, Grey Moon was ready to leave and had walked away, leaving Lone Wolf to himself. Having finished packing up the few belongings he needed, he sat looking at the place he had called home for so long now. Although sparse, the cave walls were littered with scripture he'd written in chalk and pictures he'd drawn from memories of his time with his tribe, when his parents were alive. With a heavy heart, he gently wiped the walls clean with a wet rag, knowing deep down that there was little chance of him ever returning. As he picked up his sack, he took one last look and said a prayer to his parents before following Grey Moon. Wherever he was headed, he felt sure that this was his destiny to go there; it was a chance to finally make peace with himself and avenge his parents' deaths.

On the mountain edge, Black Wolf turned to Amelia and said, 'I guess we'd better get going.' He stood and helped her to her feet. As he started to walk off to join the others, she reached for his arm, stopping him in his tracks.

'Whatever you feel, follow it through, Black Wolf. I can see there's something special about you, but you always walk away and isolate yourself. Don't keep punishing yourself for no reason; all we have is now.' She longed for him to open up to her as they stood there together.

Once more the silence hung between them as he fought against speaking his mind. 'Then we'd better go, Princess; I won't fail you again,' he replied, gently pulling her after him, his heart so full that he felt like his chest would explode.

Eventually they were all packed up. They began following the ghostly wolf back down the mountains. Grey Moon led the way quietly, the silence only broken by Lone Wolf's single question: 'So where and to whom are we headed now?'

Grey Moon was as cryptic as ever as he walked ahead. 'To the Charmed Woods, south-west of Orgent. We have three of the four, and now we need to find the fourth element — water.'

CHAPTER 25

In the Charmed Woods, the faeries were nervously awaiting their guests. Aira had spent most of the morning tidying their campsite up, then accidently knocking things over and having to start again, whilst Luna was gathering food for an evening feast and complaining that Aira was constantly getting under her feet.

Further into the woods, Ember and Tallulah were talking and getting things ready for their guests to be able to find them.

'We need to make an entrance for our visitors, otherwise they'll never find us.' Ember was instructing Tallulah and between them they were chopping a huge archway into one of the thickest thorn bushes that surrounded their home.

'I can't wait to meet them — I've been thinking about them a lot since last night.' Tallulah finished shaping the archway and sat looking at Ember.

'Why are you so interested? You're the biggest loner amongst us,' Ember asked, proudly looking at the new archway.

'I don't know, I've got a funny feeling these people will be important to me and I want to know more.'

'No change there then, Tallulah. You're always asking questions and wanting to know more.' Ember smiled to herself; she loved how inquisitive Tallulah was with everything, but always worried about her as she never seemed completely happy.

'I'm still not sure how they'll find us though... I thought these woods could never be found by outsiders?'

Ember smiled. 'Follow me and I'll show you.' She bounced off with Tallulah following behind her.

Back at their camp, Luna had got the campfire area ready and was waiting for the others to return. She'd managed to get Aira to settle down next to her but was struggling to contain her energy; she was glad to see the others return from the woods.

'It's all ready for our visitors. They have their doorway, and now all they need is a map,' Ember called out to Luna as she and Tallulah came and joined them by the fire.

Together, the four of them undertook the same kind

of elemental ritual as before, only this time the mood was lighter and Ember asked for a different sort of help.

'Our dear Great Mother, we offer you from all the elements and ask for your help. We have prepared the gateway for our visitors of magic; please guide them to us so we can receive them in peace and help them as they need. We, your children of nature, bless you and offer our love as a way of thanks.'

When Ember had finished speaking, the four of them sat and waited for the fire to die out. Instead of offering any visions this time, the steam snaked its way through the air in the direction of the newly cut entrance, and then disappeared.

'They will be here before nightfall,' announced Tallulah.

'How do you know?' replied Ember.

'This won't make any sense, but I feel it. They are very close and they have a spirit guide.' As soon as Tallulah uttered these words, they were all stopped in their tracks by the sound of a howling wolf in the distance.

***

On the outskirts of the forest, Grey Moon was mumbling a prayer as he led the group towards the woodland.

'I've heard myths of these Charmed Woods but thought them no more than stories for children. If they do exist then how do we ever hope to find them?' asked Lone Wolf, walking just behind Grey Moon.

'We won't need to, my friend. They will find us — just wait and see.'

The ghostly wolf figure stopped in the woods as if it was ready to attack something, and Grey Moon held up his hand to silence the others as they followed behind him, cracking branches and rustling leaves as they walked. All four of them stood still, watching as a strange mist floated in mid-air towards their spirit guide. As it got closer, the mist took the shape of a wolf itself and, as they watched, they briefly saw the two ghostly wolves standing nose-to-nose before the mist vanished. The remaining wolf howled loudly and then carried on walking deeper into the forest, only this time with more determination.

'They sent us a guide so we could find them; now all we

have to do is follow our friend.' Grey Moon motioned to their ghostly guide and walked after him.

Lone Wolf looked confused. 'But, I don't understand —'

'This is Grey Moon's way,' Black Wolf said, patting him on the shoulder as he passed with Amelia. 'You never understand — you just follow.'

Shaking his head, Lone Wolf followed the others into the darkening forest.

They didn't have to walk far until they reached the archway in the thick thorn bush. It seemed so obvious, here in the middle of the forest and not hidden away at all, that Lone Wolf couldn't quite believe it.

'Forgive me, Grey Moon, but I thought this place was so hidden that no one could ever find it, yet here it is, barely even concealed?'

Grey Moon smiled slightly. 'I understand your doubt, Lone Wolf. Today it is here but tomorrow it may not be. The only reason we have found it with such ease is because those who live here wanted us to. They are a charming group and blessed with much magic, but their charm is by far the biggest weapon they have. Normal people believe what these folk want them to believe, but they have chosen to invite us here. Come now, my friends, let's not keep them waiting.' He stepped over the threshold and out of sight, slowly followed by the others.

Stepping out onto the mossy land beyond the gateway, it was like day had become night. The woods were suddenly very dark, but there were thousands of twinkling lights lining a path for them to follow. The magical glow led all the way into a clearing where the land was flatter and more open, and as they walked along they could hear beautiful singing in the distance.

The two groups noticed each other at almost exactly the same time, the faeries looking up from their fire and the travellers looking down from the fallen tree stump they were facing, slightly higher in the woods.

'Greetings, ladies, and thank you for guiding us here,' Grey Moon said. 'I am Grey Moon and these are my companions, Lone Wolf, Black Wolf and Amelia, a princess from the great walled city. We come seeking help.'

'Who are these people?' Amelia whispered to Black Wolf, who shrugged at her, looking as confused as she was.

'These are the faery folk, Princess,' Lone Wolf replied, 'but be careful because they are far more powerful than they look, and twice as mischievous.'

'You are all most welcome. Come sit by the fire and rest your aching bodies. We would be honoured to host you tonight and assist if we can. I am Luna and these are my relatives, Ember, Aira and Tallulah.'

Amelia couldn't help but stare at their beautiful outfits, all made from natural materials of the oddest variety; even things like dry leaves and moss had been used. They were dressed in different shades of green and blended in with their surroundings perfectly.

As the group sat down around the fire, leaning their backs against the fallen tree stump, they all greeted each other and exchanged pleasantries. Aira squealed with excitement, hugging everyone, whilst Luna handed out forest-made drinks in carved wooden cups. Ember quietly tried to observe these strangers while Tallulah, as usual, sat silently in the shadows, keeping herself to herself.

'We can have a feast tonight and celebrate the company of others — something we never do. Then you can tell us all why you are here and what we can do to help you,' Ember announced.

'That sounds wonderful, child. We've had a long trek with no rest today. There is lots to discuss, too,' replied Grey Moon.

Ember was satisfied that the visitors were harmless and wanted to make them feel comfortable. 'If any of you need to freshen up, there is a stream a bit farther on, which feeds the Lake of Essence. Feel free to use the running water from the waterfall, if you wish.'

'I'd like to. Could show me where to go, please?' Black Wolf said, standing up, desperate to clean the dirt and dust from his face.

'Certainly, Black Wolf, Tallulah will show you.' Ember smiled as Tallulah got up and led him away from the group.

Reaching the flowing water, Black Wolf cupped his hands and started to splash his face clean. His guide had been so quiet the whole time that it made him feel nervous, so he tried to make conversation.

'You have a beautiful home here. I hope we haven't upset you all by disturbing your peace?' he said, trying to shake himself dry.

'Here, use this,' said Tallulah, handing him some sort of handmade cloth. As their hands touched briefly, Black Wolf felt his heart beat wildly in his chest as visions of Esmee flew into his mind.

'I must go,' Tallulah stammered and ran back to the others, leaving Black Wolf kneeling alone at the stream, trying to hold back the tears that wanted to pour out of him.

He tried to speak but couldn't; he was powerless to do anything but watch her disappear into the woods.

CHAPTER 26

The people of Orgent were cowering under the control of their captor as the night seemed to grow colder and darker around them. They had witnessed death and invasion, and now they were powerless to do anything as Elspeth was brutally degraded before their eyes.

The evil intruder hadn't spoken in a while; instead he watched Elspeth's body hanging in the air as it was slowly disrobed. The emperor had stopped begging for her to be spared, as he knew it would just serve to anger his opponent even more.

The evil being approached her body as he spoke. 'Have I not convinced you to help me yet, child? Is your princess so precious to you that you would continue to suffer just to help her?'

'I would rather die than help you!' Elspeth spat back at him. 'There is nothing you can do to make me change my mind!'

'I *will* kill you, girl, trust me — but allow me to indulge myself first. It has been a long time for me, lying in wait, and I'm enjoying the display of innocent flesh.' He turned to the crowd, cowering by their doors, and bellowed at them, 'Who wants to see more?!'

As the emperor shouted 'no!' the vile being dragged his claw-like fingers through the air, his magic tearing the last of the maid's dress to shreds and casting it aside.

Naked and shivering, Elspeth cried out loudly and tried to plead with him. 'Please, just stop, I cannot help you anyway. I don't know where the princess is, so I couldn't tell you even if I wanted to! I'm of no use to you.'

'You underestimate yourself, girl. You are far more useful to me than you think. You seem reluctant to help me though, so maybe you need some convincing?'

As the evil being's black smoke swept away from her, Elspeth watched it snake around the courtyard, as if searching for something, before finally it flew at a figure in the dark and dragged them out into the open, dumping them at her feet.

Elspeth stared in horror as the face of this person was revealed to her, and she screamed at the stranger, 'No, please don't touch her! She is nothing to do with this.'

'But she is your mother; I think she has everything to do with this.' And the stranger laughed as he used his powers to squeeze the life from the woman.

'Time is short, dear Elspeth. Your mother's life or your help? The choice is yours.'

'Don't help him...' her mother croaked, unable to speak as her throat tightened. She could barely breathe.

'Stop, I beg you! Let my mother go and I'll help you!' Elspeth screamed, finally defeated by this dark power that seemed intent on destroying anything that stood in its way.

'Elspeth, don't...' her mother managed to say before she was sent flying across the floor and back into the shadows.

'You have chosen well, child. Now, there is one thing I need from you, and trust me, if you give it to me I will let your family live.'

'What do you want?' the maid asked, the tears flowing down her face.

'Your body,' the evil being said coldly, and with a flick of his hand he sent a stream of thick, dark smoke from within him, across the gap between them, and down her throat.

The emperor watched in terror as the smoke disappeared inside her, making her gag and choke, until she fell still and her head slumped forward.

'You promised you wouldn't kill her! What kind of sick creature are you?' the emperor yelled.

'I am what you all fear the most, Emperor. Those hidden desires every man holds deep down within him. I am what you are all too afraid to be: true power. Anyway, your daughter's slave isn't dead; go see for yourself.' With this, the dark power released the emperor and let Elspeth drop to the ground at the same time.

The emperor ran over to the girl's body and knelt next to her. 'Elspeth, are you alright? I'm here, I won't let him hurt you again,' he said as he removed his robe and tried to cover her with it.

She sat bolt upright and stared at him, her eyes glowing an eerie shade of red, and she spoke with a gravelly tone. 'I'm fine, Emperor, I don't need to be protected from him — and he's right... You should join with us and make the whole kingdom ours.'

'You don't know what you're saying, child. This thing is pure evil and we need to get away from it.' The emperor was shocked by her strange behaviour and moved back from her slightly.

'You have nothing to fear, Emperor. I have been liberated, woken from my sleep, and I can help you.' She shrugged the robe off her shoulders, letting him see her naked flesh, and moved closer to him. 'It's been a long time since your queen left us... You must get lonely... Maybe I can help you find some happiness again?' She took his hand, placed it on her chest and leant in to kiss him.

'What are you doing?' he said in alarm, pushing her away and scrambling to his feet. He turned to the evil being, shaking with anger. 'What have you done to her? Who is this monstrosity you've put before me?'

'I told you I wouldn't kill her, Emperor. But I also told you if she didn't help me, I'd make her in my image.' He laughed loudly. He turned to one of the guards and used his power to take his sword from his sheath and drop it at Elspeth's feet. 'I don't think the emperor trusts your plans, child... Maybe you need to convince him.'

Elspeth picked up the sword and stood before the emperor, still naked. 'Maybe I should make you my queen then, if you're not man enough to take me?' she sneered, before turning the sword so it was pointing towards her own face.

The emperor panicked and looked towards the cruel stranger again. 'You said you wouldn't hurt her, please just stop this!'

'*I* won't hurt her... It's what she'll do to herself that you need to worry about now.'

When the evil being had finished speaking, the emperor turned back to Elspeth to find she had pressed the tip of the sword so heavily against her skin that a small bead of blood had appeared.

'Are you sure you don't want me, Emperor?' she taunted him. 'Shall I destroy myself instead?'

'Elspeth, please stop, I'll do whatever I can to protect you. Just put the sword down and we can talk.' He knew he was running out of chances to stop her from hurting herself.

'The choice is yours, Emperor: accept me as your new queen, or I might as well end myself now.' The question hung in the air. Suddenly, the emperor was powerless to help as Elspeth drew the sword slowly down her cheek.

CHAPTER 27

When Black Wolf returned to the others by the fire, he noticed Tallulah was back in the shadows, sitting quietly and avoiding eye contact with him. Luna was cooking food but Grey Moon had got more out of his bag for his tribe to eat. He'd explained to the others quietly that no humans should ever eat faery food, as the magic they possess seeps into the food itself when they prepare it, leaving the person unable to survive on anything other than faery food once they've sampled it.

'I see the knowledge of our charms, as well as our food, is known to you,' Luna said to him cheekily.

'I mean you no offence, I promise,' Grey Moon replied, placing their food separately on the fire. 'But we cannot afford to be trapped in your presence, no matter how beautiful you or your home are.'

'I understand, Grey Moon; we will be on our best behaviour, I promise.' Luna winked at him, smiling, as she handed out her food to the faeries.

As they sat eating, Grey Moon and Amelia told their hosts everything about the troubles at Orgent and how the roots of this problem stretched back a long way into the past. The faeries listened to every word with furrowed brows, trying to understand the madness going on in the world around them. When they had finished the story, Ember was the first to speak.

'I sensed that something had changed in the world around us, but I never realised how serious it was. We are in a world of our own making here. How can we be of any use to you?' she questioned, feeling confused.

Grey Moon spoke to Ember but looked curiously at all of the faeries, trying to work out which one he might need. 'As I said, our Great Mother split the power four ways and we have discovered three of these powers. They all match the elements with their own individual, hidden talents, and we have come here in search of the fourth power. Once we find it, we can go and save Orgent and restore natural order to all of the lands.'

'Do you know which of us the chosen one is?' Tallulah said quietly, looking up nervously at Black Wolf.

Black Wolf reached into his sack and passed the box to Grey Moon. The fourth light was glowing bright green and it confirmed to him that they were definitely in the presence of the final power they needed.

'We can find out easily enough if the four of you will allow me to perform one of my people's ancient rituals,' Grey Moon replied, getting more of his paste and herbs out from his sack, ready to get the answer.

The faeries all looked towards Luna and she nodded in agreement. 'We trust you, and our Great Mother wouldn't have allowed you here otherwise, so we will do what you need and let her magic reveal the answer,' she said to him.

'Thank you, Luna. It won't take long and I promise it is safe.' Grey Moon dabbed the paste on all four of the faeries' foreheads and threw a heap of herbs into the fire.

Everyone sat around the fire waiting for something to happen; the faeries all looked nervously at each other — then Tallulah slumped to the floor. Aira moved towards her to help, but Luna grabbed her arm. 'It's okay — leave her and she'll return when she's ready, I promise.'

They all watched as Tallulah's body twitched slightly, as if she was dreaming, and they knew she was on a strange journey that only she could reveal once she was awake again.

Eventually she woke, her eyes wide and staring, before scrambling to her feet and fleeing into the woods.

'Tallulah!' Ember called after her, but she was already gone.

'I'll go and talk to her — you wait here,' Black Wolf said hastily, and he headed off after her.

When he caught up with her, she was sitting at the base of the tree overlooking the Lake of Essence. Black Wolf kept his distance, not wanting to scare her. 'Tallulah, are you okay? Did you want to talk about it?'

She looked up at him, her eyes full of sorrow, 'Do you know what this tree is?' she said.

'No, I know very little of your world,' he replied, feeling lost in his surroundings.

'This is the wolf tree and it is said to hold a very sacred power. Its lifeblood is taken directly from the Lake of Essence. For as long as I can remember, I have sat here alone, feeling like something was missing from my life and always longing to know why. Now I know why this place has always meant so much to me and why I've always felt saddened by its name. I was the one waiting for a wolf, and now he is here.'

'Is it really you, my child?' Black Wolf asked nervously, unable to believe what he hoped was true.

'It is,' she said. 'I saw it all in the visions. I love my faery family and always will, but I longed for more, for something I never even knew existed until now.'

Black Wolf fought back the emotions rising in him as he spoke again. 'What is it you longed for, Tallulah?'

'You,' she said. She then uttered two words that both broke and fixed his heart with equal measure. 'My father.' As she spoke those words, she ran towards him and threw herself against his body, sobbing loudly.

'Hush now, it's okay, my child, I'm here. I won't leave you again, I promise.' He pulled her closer into him and softly kissed the top of her hair, inhaling her beautiful scent.

'Then it's true?' she asked. 'I'm the chosen one you all spoke of? I'll be going with you to Orgent?' Her tears had started to subside, replaced instead by typically infectious faery excitement.

'Yes, child, you are the one. You need to speak to Grey Moon and your family, though, then we can start planning.'

'I'll go speak to them now. I'll see you back at the fire,' Tallulah said, suddenly full of energy, before kissing him on the cheek and bouncing off back to the others, leaving a bemused Black Wolf stood alone, looking into the lake.

'Is that her?' Amelia's voice broke the silence and she stepped quietly out of the woods and joined him.

'Yes, Princess, she's the one,' he said, a solitary tear rolling down his cheek.

'Our daughter...' Amelia whispered, amazed at how much those two words made her feel.

'But she's not though, is she?' Black Wolf said furiously. 'And there is no us — it has all gone and we cannot get it back. Time has moved on but we are all stuck, frozen in time and aching with loss.' The tears came hard now as he pulled his knife from his pocket and cut his hand open. '*This* is real — here and now. The blood, the pain... Everything else is just a ghost of another age.' He threw the knife in anger and it stuck deep in the base of the wolf tree, where

Tallulah had been sitting.

Amelia stepped closer to him. 'Remember what Grey Moon said? Sometimes you can live in each other's hearts for a lifetime and it still takes time for the souls to recognise each other when you meet as strangers. We don't need to chase ghosts; it's what we feel now that matters.' She took his injured hand and tried to stop the blood flowing from it by ripping a part of her dress off and soaking it in the lake.

'When I look at you, I feel alive, Princess. Every part of me wants to be with you, but how can I tell if it's real or not?' He wiped the tears away and his eyes burned into hers.

'Is this real?' she said, stroking his face. 'Or this...' She leant towards him, kissing him passionately, their body heat combining as they were lost in a moment that had been building for a lifetime. Together they knelt down, hungrily reaching for each other, unaware that the mystical lights around them faded before eventually disappearing, leaving them together in the dark with just their combined silhouette reflecting off of the moonlit lake.

***

Back at the campfire, Tallulah had returned and told the others what she'd seen; they'd barely been able to get a word in as she'd babbled excitedly at them all.

Luna looked concerned as she finally got the chance to speak. 'But you know nothing of the outside world, Tallulah — none of us do. This all sounds very dangerous and I cannot accept you leaving here. You could get hurt!'

'But we all saw the vision of what will happen if this power isn't stopped. The forests will be destroyed and we'd all die anyway.' Tallulah was desperate not to miss her chance for an adventure, even if it was dangerous.

After a long, thoughtful pause, Ember spoke. 'She's right, Luna, and we've always felt like she wasn't truly happy or fulfilling her potential here. I think we need to let her go and pray that this works, for all our sakes.'

'You have my word that I'll protect her in every way I can and this really is our only chance of any of us surviving,' Grey Moon chipped in. 'Once we have defeated the evil, Tallulah will be free to do what she wishes.'

'Please, Luna, it's my destiny, I'm sure it is,' said Tallulah.

Realising that this wasn't an argument she could win, Luna finally bowed backed down and nodded.

Tallulah squealed in excitement and hugged Luna. 'Thank you, Luna. I'll be fine, I know I will. I have Black Wolf and Grey Moon to protect me, and Lone Wolf too of course — he's a brave warrior,' she said, looking at Lone Wolf and realising he needed to know how important he was.

'It's an honour, Tallulah — it always was,' Lone Wolf said to her, smiling.

'We are all agreed then,' said Grey Moon. 'We leave for Orgent at first light.'

By the lake, the twinkling lights were back, and Black Wolf and Amelia were lying together by the lake, smiling for the first time since they'd met.

He spoke gently in her ear. 'As much as I want to stay here, I guess we need to get back to the others.'

'I know… We'd better find them before they come and find us.' She giggled and made sure her dress was intact before getting to her feet.

As she brushed the leaves from her dress, Black Wolf walked over to the tree and pulled the knife out. As he did so, the cut on his hand healed itself before his eyes. 'This place is very strange,' he said, showing Amelia his hand. As he did so, he noticed blood running down her cheek. 'You're bleeding, Princess! What happened?'

As he moved towards her, she slumped to the floor, murmuring, 'Elspeth…'

Panicking, Black Wolf threw her over his shoulder and carried her back to the others, where he laid her down by the fire and dabbed her face with a wet cloth.

'There's no cut, Grey Moon. Where did all the blood come from?'

Grey Moon held some strong scented herbs under her nose and she woke up immediately, looking dazed but unhurt. 'What happened, Princess?'

'I don't know… I saw Elspeth's face — she's my maid — and then I felt like I was choking and I had blood on me. It was really frightening. I felt so cold.'

Grey Moon looked serious as he spoke. 'All of the four have individual powers, Princess. You are air and your power is empathy. I fear you are getting feelings from your home.'

'What can we do?' Amelia asked, apprehension growing within her.

'Nothing yet, my child, but it means we don't have long. We must rest and leave as soon as it is light. It will take us another day to gather our people and get to Orgent, but we cannot take longer than that.'

'We have faery blankets you can use, and we'll wake you early,' Luna said to the group, and she headed off to fetch the bedding.

'Don't worry, Princess. Tomorrow we will save your people,' Black Wolf said, lying next to her and holding her close.

'Thank you, Black Wolf. You are a true warrior and I owe you everything. Can I ask that you do just one thing for me though?' she asked, curling into him.

'Anything you ask.'

'Call me Amelia,' she said, smiling to herself and holding his hands tightly around her waist.

The faeries moved off to their own sleeping areas, nestled deep in the hollow trunks of the larger trees, invisible to the naked eye — all except for Tallulah, who lay down close to Lone Wolf. 'I need a brave warrior to keep me safe,' she said to him, smiling shyly.

'Again, it would be an honour,' he replied. He stayed awake for a while, watching the lights around them fade.

Before Grey Moon settled, he threw some more herbs into the fire and spoke quietly to himself. 'Let us sleep, Great Mother. All your children are together again, and tomorrow we will banish this evil and bring peace to your home once more.'

As the herbs crackled and hissed in the fire, a beautiful perfumed smoke spread around the camp, sending them all into a blissfully peaceful sleep.

CHAPTER 28

Majila ran as fast as he could up the huge white steps of the palace. The whole of the city had descended into chaos and people were running everywhere, some looking to escape and others looking for a place to hide.

The dark force that had wiped out Majila's tribe had somehow discovered where he was hiding, and that morning they had attacked without warning. The marketplace was still awash with bodies of murdered traders and Majila had been told that these evil men were headed to the palace to speak to Drei Ran. Earlier that morning, the children had all gone to the temple for lessons and Majila knew time was running out for him to find Esmee before they did. Together, they had to escape.

He made his way up the steps, struggling against the surge of people running in the opposite direction. Majila recalled his conversation with Drei Ran, remembering all he had been told about this city living in peace and having no fighters. Majila hadn't even been able to find Kaliam, so it was just him and his sword against a force that could seemingly destroy anything and everything with ease.

Majila made it to the second level of the palace steps and stopped to get his breath back. Nearby, two women were huddled together, praying. When they saw him they stopped and stared angrily, whispering to each other and pointing their fingers at him. Majila walked over to the women, holding his hands up to show them he wasn't a threat.

'Can you tell me where to find the children? Please, I need to find my daughter — she is in great danger.'

'Don't you think you've done enough already? You never should have come here,' one of the women hissed at Majila.

'I haven't done anything — all I want is to find my daughter. Please help me, I'm begging you. I don't know why any of this is happening.' Majila sensed that his chances of finding Esmee were getting smaller all the time.

'Don't you see? This is all your fault. They are here because of you!' The woman threw herself at Majila, hitting him repeatedly in the chest until her friend pulled her away and down the steps. She was still screaming at him as they ran. 'You have killed us all! You are a curse!'

Majila stood watching the women flee down the steps. Their anger had shocked him and the same guilt from the events at his camp washed over him again. He dusted himself down and carried on up the next set of steps. As bad as he felt, he knew he couldn't change things now. He could only hope to save Esmee and escape.

When he reached the main walkway to the palace, Majila saw two guards outside the main doors. They were both dressed completely in black and had swords hanging down from their belts. There were people scattered everywhere around them, some crouching down in fear, some slowly trying to escape and others lying dead on the floor. Slowly, Majila crept towards the guards, using the mass of bodies as cover. They were both stood with their backs to him and, as he got closer, he knew his best chance was to attack now. Majila crept closer to the guards, slowly drawing his sword in readiness. He picked up a rock and, when he was close enough, he threw it along the floor, creating a distraction and so he could gain an advantage in the fight.

As one of the guards moved forward to investigate the noise, Majila leapt to his feet. He jumped forward, kicking the moving guard in the back whilst plunging his sword deep into the other guard's chest. One guard fell forward onto his knees, dropping his sword as he did so, and the other guard contorted in agony before Majila withdrew his sword, causing him to slump lifelessly to the ground.

The guard on the floor was trying to get back to his feet, and as he staggered forward he grabbed his sword and turned to face Majila. His face looked a deathly shade of grey and his eyes bore deep into Majila's, who could feel the evil pouring out of him.

'Your resistance is pointless; you will never escape — and neither will your daughter!' the guard snarled.

Majila stood tall, ready to fight with all he had left in him. 'I will fight to the death trying. You will not take my daughter.'

Without another word, the guard lunged at Majila with his sword. Visions of all the destruction caused by these people filled his mind as he deflected the blow with his own sword and circled round the guard, his own sword cutting through the air and forcing his opponent back on his heels. The two fighters exchanged heavy blows, the sound of the clashing swords echoing loudly along the temple walls. Gaining the advantage, Majila threw his weight towards the guard, but as he stepped towards where the other guard's fallen body had been, something caught his eye and momentarily distracted him. The guard took this opportunity to attack and struck the sword from Majila's hand before pinning him against the wall, one hand around his throat and the sword pointed at his chest.

'Remember this view, Majila, for it is the last thing you'll ever see. I want you to know that you have failed as I kill you. First you failed your people, and now you have failed your daughter.'

The panic rose in Majila and he closed his eyes, desperately trying to visualise Esmee escaping. He could do nothing now but wait for the sword to pierce his chest and allow the darkness to envelop him. But, just as he was expecting the worst, he suddenly felt the hand loosen from around his throat and he heard the clatter of a sword against the stone floor.

'You are safe, my friend. You didn't think I would miss a fight, did you? Now, follow me and we'll go save Esmee.'

Majila opened his eyes to see Kaliam wiping blood from his sword. The body of the dead guard lay on the floor between them.

Majila dropped to his knees, struggling to comprehend what had happened. He slowly regained his composure, and picked up his sword. Standing, he turned to his friend. 'I owe you my life. Thank you, Kaliam. Who are these people?'

'I think the question is not who, but what,' said Kaliam as he looked at the body of the slain soldier, slowly turning to ashes before their eyes.

'I saw the other body disintegrate and I hesitated. If you hadn't saved me I'd be dead by now.'

'Majila, we don't have time for these things now. Follow me; I think I know where Esmee is.' Kaliam put his hand on Majila's shoulder before leading him through the door in the temple wall. All Majila could do was follow, and pray that it wasn't too late.

CHAPTER 29

Most of the group felt really refreshed when they woke the next morning; whatever Grey Moon had thrown in the fire had helped them to relax. The faeries were busy fussing around Tallulah, packing food and other supplies in a sack for her, whilst Grey Moon was checking Amelia was feeling alright after her shock the night before.

However, Black Wolf and Lone Wolf had woken uncomfortably from the same dream. They walked to the waterfall together to freshen up before their next trek, discussing what they'd seen in their dreams.

Lone Wolf felt the need to be honest if they were stepping into battle together. 'I'm finding it so difficult to deal with what we're learning, Black Wolf. I don't believe I'm any more of a warrior than you are but I don't want to let you down.'

'You won't let anyone down — we all believe in you,' said Black Wolf. 'Did you see what I saw last night? That was the second time you saved my life, and the help you gave a complete stranger was a bravery that I've never witnessed before, or since. This is all so strange, I know, but you must believe in yourself.' Black Wolf realised it was the first time they'd really spoken since meeting and wanted to let Lone Wolf know that he was a vital part of their team.

'Thank you, Black Wolf. I saw what you saw too, and if this is the same evil we will face at Orgent then I fear for us all. I just hope that Grey Moon's prophecies about our combined powers are true.'

'I'm sure Grey Moon is right. It will be difficult but I have to believe we can defeat it. It's all we can do — and trust me, I wouldn't want to face you.' Black Wolf smiled and patted Lone Wolf on the back. 'Just don't run off and leave me to play at being a nanny this time,' he added, laughing.

Lone Wolf pushed Black Wolf into the lake. 'That'll teach you!' he said, walking off back to camp, leaving Black Wolf laughing to himself, knee-deep in the water.

'I thought *I* was supposed to be the child!' a voice called, and Tallulah appeared. 'We're nearly ready, so you'd better join us,' she said, guiding Black Wolf back to camp.

A short while later, everyone was packed and ready to

go, and the task that lay ahead of the group weighed heavily on their minds. Black Wolf sat with Amelia, fussing over her wellbeing. Tallulah crept up beside them.

'I'm alright, Black Wolf, honestly, I feel fine today,' Amelia said. 'I'm just worried about my father and Elspeth, but we'll be heading off to rescue them soon.' She kissed him and finished packing stuff into a sack. Suddenly she felt arms round her, squeezing hard. 'I won't be alright if you squeeze the life out of me before we head off,' she said to Tallulah, ruffling her hair and hiding how strange it was to feel motherly towards this quirky stranger.

'Sorry. I just wanted to let you know how excited I am to have met you,' the faery replied, releasing her grip slightly.

'That's alright, Tallulah, I know. Once we're safe we'll have time to talk and get to know each other.'

'I'd like that,' replied Tallulah. She then disappeared amongst the other faeries.

'She's quite a character,' Black Wolf said proudly, watching her go.

'She certainly is,' agreed Amelia. 'I often wondered what it would be like to have a child.'

Black Wolf noticed her sad tone and hugged her closer. 'One day you'll find out, Amelia. You'll have not just a child but the future emperor — now *there's* pressure for you.' He smiled at her but the air was tinged with sadness as they both thought about what could have been, if their lives hadn't been destroyed in the past by such horrific events.

'We should start our journey now,' Grey Moon called out to the group, after saying his goodbyes to the faeries.

Lone Wolf and Amelia said quick goodbyes and followed Grey Moon back to the archway, leaving Black Wolf and Tallulah still at camp.

'Thank you for welcoming us. I hope to see you again soon,' Black Wolf said, bowing before the other three faeries.

'Make sure you look after our girl,' Luna said to him.

'I promise to return her safely,' he said, before turning to Tallulah. 'I'll leave you to say your goodbyes.' He followed the others.

'I trust you, Tallulah; I know this is what you need and I hope you find everything you wished for. Travel well, my sister,' said Ember, handing her a small pouch.

'We will pray for our Great Mother to bring you back

safely. You have my blessing,' said Luna.

'Bring me back a nice faery prince!' said Aira, jumping at Tallulah and hugging her tightly whilst trying to hold back the tears.

Tallulah herself was choking back the tears as she spoke, 'Thank you for everything you've done for me. I love you all and will see you again one day.'

The four of them hugged and then Tallulah joined her new friends at the archway. 'I'm ready,' she said to Grey Moon. With Black Wolf's arm round her shoulder, they all stepped through the gap and out of the Charmed Woods.

CHAPTER 30

The mood in Orgent had grown even darker after Elspeth had cut herself with the sword. The emperor was stood watching, in a state of shock, as the blood spilled down her body, making her look almost demonic in the eerie light, with her red eyes.

Elspeth spoke to the evil being in an almost trance-like state. 'The message was received, my lord. I know that the princess felt my pain and I'm sure she will worry now.'

'Good. Now you can all pray that she arrives sooner rather than later, or more of you will have to pay for her lack of urgency.'

The emperor had slumped to the floor, head in hands, fighting back the tears; he was desperate not to show his opponent any weakness.

'You're very quiet there, Emperor. Are you not enjoying the show I've put on for your celebrations? Maybe we need some more excitement?' The vile being goaded the emperor, laughing wickedly at the wreck of a man before him.

'Why don't you just take me and let all of these people go free? Please, I beg of you...'

'Don't you see, Emperor? I can't take you. Your spirit is not broken like that servant girl's; you still have too much fight in you, too much anger. You'll be here until the end of this, believe me — and you will hand me your kingdom on a plate.'

Suddenly the emperor heard a sobbing and he realised it was coming from Elspeth, so he rushed over to her and put his arms round her, hugging her tightly to him. He spoke softly in her ear. 'You've come back, Elspeth! It's a miracle. Don't cry, my dear, I'll keep you safe.'

'Will you keep me warm too?' she replied huskily, grabbing his head and rubbing her blood-soaked lips against his. 'I need a man who can show me what true power is, Emperor. Make me your queen,' she hissed, the blood spilling over his robes as he tried to hold her away from him.

The anger in the emperor surfaced as he shouted at the evil intruder. 'Get her away from me! Lies and trickery!

You will pay for all this, mark my words — this kingdom will crush you.'

'Crushed, by whom? You bore me, Emperor. Maybe we can give your guards a chance, and if they defeat me then you can all walk free.' The stranger looked at the few guards dotted around the courtyard and picked the five he thought looked the most powerful. He signalled to his ghostly army and, one by one, they brought all five forward and stood them before the stranger. 'Come and get me,' he challenged them.

The guards looked at the emperor, who nodded to them, and then drew their swords, all five pointed towards the evil figure. They kept their formation with the lead guard at the front, and moved towards their foe. The evil being stood before them, his arms aloft, with wispy trails of black ash almost invisibly wafting out of him, towards the guards.

'Five...' the stranger said aloud.

With this, one of the two guards at the back suddenly swung his sword towards his friend, beheading him almost instantly.

'Four...'

The same guard thrust his sword through the spine of the man in front of him, the bloody body dropping on the spot.

'Three...'

The guard spun north-west and sliced the second guard from throat to groin, blood and guts tipping out under the feet of the head guard who had now spun round and was facing the swordsman head on.

'Two...'

The guard slit his own throat and the head guard watched as his eyes turned from red back to brown again and blood flooded from the wound on his neck.

'We all know what comes next, don't we, Emperor?' the evil being laughed. 'One...'

With that word, he thrust his hand towards the head guard, choking him in mid-air. The guard's skin blistered and turned to black ash, spilling on the floor of the courtyard.

'I don't think you'll be crushing me, do you, Emperor?' he taunted, seeming to grow in stature with every death.

The emperor stood up and walked over to the stranger, defiantly staring at him as he spoke. 'If you say my spirit is not broken then face *me*, one on one, and leave all these innocent people out of this.'

'There is no such thing as innocence, Emperor — you should know that more than anyone here. Once a coward, always a coward. In every life you live, you make a choice, and each time your choice has helped me — yet you always seem to end up living in temples? Fortune does seem to favour the weak.'

The emperor was enraged by the accusations. 'I've never met you before. These are all more lies — this is more trickery!'

'You will see in time. It's funny how a temple of yours can turn away a father and child, yet in the next life, you hope they come and rescue you,' said the stranger, glaring at the emperor. For a brief moment, the emperor felt a guilt deep inside him like never before, and he could have sworn he saw a vision in those red eyes. A vision of a dark cloud, floating away from a bright white temple and a small blonde child, dotted with blood, huddled together with other children by a forest.

CHAPTER 31

After stepping through the archway, the group had found themselves right on the outskirts of the forest, so they had less distance to travel than when they had headed there from the mountains.

'Your folk really are quite magical aren't they?' Lone Wolf said to Tallulah as they walked along, side by side.

'We have our uses,' she replied, grinning to herself. 'So are you my own personal guard now, then? Have you sworn an oath to protect me at all costs?'

'Nothing quite as formal as that, but in the past I told someone I'd help find and protect their daughter, so that's what I'm doing now, in a way.' Struggling to work out the sense in all this, his answer confused him more than anyone.

'You mean my father?' Tallulah asked.

'To be honest, I'm not really sure how any of this works. But in a way, I guess so, yes.'

'What are you thinking about?' she asked, staring up at him curiously.

'I think you ask too many questions,' he said, smiling, and playfully nudged her with his shoulder.

Further behind them, Black Wolf and Amelia walked together, watching Tallulah wearing Lone Wolf out.

'What will you do when all this is over?' the princess asked.

'If we survive, then I'll return to the lowlands and lead my people, I guess. One day I'll have to take Grey Moon's place, so I've still got lots to learn.' Black Wolf paused. 'What will you do?'

'There will have to be changes at Orgent, so I'll have to speak to my father about it. We need to be allowed to voyage into the night world again, but with some form of protection. I was hoping Grey Moon might help us and we could open our gates more, for your people, if you needed us. I'd like to build a better relationship with the tribesmen.' She blushed slightly as she spoke.

'I think a tribesman would be honoured by your wish to help,' he replied, and they carried on without mentioning anything more about the future. They had scars from the past, and in the present there was grave danger. So, to them, any future was just a dream.

Ahead of them all, Grey Moon was leading the way. He was glad that the group were enjoying each other's company, as it gave him some time to be alone and gather his thoughts. The conversation with Black Wolf back at the mountains had shaken him up and he knew it wouldn't be long before he'd have to tell him more about his early days, but he could only hope that for the moment, at least, more revelations could be delayed.

The walk had been a lot easier with the help of the faeries, and it wasn't long before they arrived at a clearing, which had the same river running through it that the faery camp had. On the other side of this river was a long path uphill that headed to Orgent. The path was through the woodland that surrounded the land lower than Orgent, but so many trees had been felled here that the route was fairly easy to trek up. The only problem in the walk up the path would be the lack of cover available for the group; this was made worse by the fact that the path headed straight to Orgent, which overlooked it from a great height.

'We need to call the others before we continue,' said Grey Moon, stopping before the river and unpacking things from his sack.

'How are we going to do that?' asked Lone Wolf.

'One of our ancient smoke rituals, my friend, and you're just the person I need to help me.' Grey Moon patted the floor next to him, inviting his friend to join him.

'Looks like we're not needed,' said Amelia to Black Wolf, who seemed strangely preoccupied.

'I guess not,' he replied, sitting near the others and staring into the distance.

Grey Moon had got everything ready, and Lone Wolf had started a strong fire near the river. The wood was already burning fiercely, the flames dancing high into the air above them, and he was sat with a handful of the herbs that Grey Moon had given him.

Sat by the fire, Grey Moon started to chant, softly at first, and then slowly growing louder. Lone Wolf had witnessed this sort of ceremony before and hummed along to the chanting, leaving Grey Moon free to stop and address his people.

'Children of my land, I pray that our Great Mother lets

my voice be heard by you. The time has come for the action we spoke of, and we need your strength behind us. Let the angry fire of war guide you to us before next light and we will claim back peace for all our people.' Grey Moon nodded to Lone Wolf, who threw the herbs into the fire. The flame and smoke instantly turned a deep red and sent the signal they needed.

'Now we wait,' Grey Moon said to his friend, and Lone Wolf watched as the fire worked its magic, right in front of him.

Across the clearing, the other three were sat together. Black Wolf still quiet. Tallulah twirled the small pouch Ember had given her in her hands.

'What have you got there?' enquired Amelia.

'This is a special bag of faery dust that will help me find the Charmed Woods again, if I need to return,' she replied.

'If?' said Amelia, 'Once we've saved Orgent, you'll be free to return home, Tallulah, then life can return to normal again.'

'I guess,' Tallulah mumbled, looking down at the floor.

'What's wrong, Tallulah? You don't seem very happy about that.'

'I've spent my whole life waiting for more and now I've found it, with you and Black Wolf. I guess I was hoping we might all be able to stay together, once this is over...' She looked at Black Wolf, but he didn't appear to have heard them.

'There's a lot to do before we worry about that though. We'll work that all out when we're safe, don't worry.' Amelia put her arm round Tallulah and hugged her, trying to offer her some comfort.

'We're all connected, but we need to try to leave the past behind us. It's time for us to create a new connection and if it is meant to be, then we'll always be close,' Black Wolf said, still staring into the distance. He wanted nothing more than to keep both of them close, now he'd found them again, but he knew in his heart that things could never be the same again.

The two women looked at each other and smiled; they had all found each other after so long — maybe he was right and it would all work out, one way or another.

'I'll be back later. Don't go getting in any trouble,' Black

Wolf said to them, before wandering over to look at the fire.

'We have called for the others and they should arrive by nightfall,' Grey Moon said to him. 'You're welcome to sit with us if you wish, my child.'

Black Wolf sat next to the warrior and the teacher, mesmerised by the flame and staring at it until a strange vision appeared to him from deep within the heart of the fire.

He saw the tree stump from the start of his days again and, as he watched, a wolf appeared out of the top and ran off into the distance. Black Wolf watched the scene change to a great battle, where he was sure he saw Grey Moon fall during the fight, and then the wolf kept running. The wolf finally reached a huge cloaked figure and with its teeth bared, snarling, it leapt straight at the figure and appeared to disappear into it, until everything vanished without a trace.

'What is it, my child?' Grey Moon asked, looking concerned at his friend.

'Nothing, I'm just tired,' said Black Wolf, unable to tell Grey Moon what he'd just seen. As he sat there, it occurred to him he'd spent so long worrying about Amelia and Tallulah that he'd never thought Grey Moon could be lost in this battle.

'So what is our next move?' said Lone Wolf.

'We need to cross this river and our people will meet us if we wait for them farther up the hill on the other side.

'That's easy,' said Tallulah, who had wandered over to join them, with Amelia by her side.

'You'd better show us then,' said Lone Wolf, trying to hide the scorn from his voice, and the group watched as Tallulah walked across the river, without her feet even entering the water.

'See,' she called back from the other side, 'things are only as difficult as you make them.'

'Let's go then,' said Lone Wolf, hoisting his sack onto his back, and hopping onto the river.

'Lone Wolf, wait!' called Grey Moon, but it was already too late, and with a huge splash, Lone Wolf was on his back in the water, muttering angrily, whilst the others laughed amongst themselves.

'I was going to remind you of the faeries' trickery and charm,' said Grey Moon, stifling a laugh.

'People see what we want them to see,' said Tallulah

cheekily.

'I'll remember that,' Lone Wolf replied, narrowing his eyes as he got to his feet, and for a brief moment the laughter overtook the fear and the strange group of travellers crossed the river together, smiling to themselves.

CHAPTER 32

In Orgent, the emperor was still reeling from the vision he'd seen reflected in the stranger's eyes. Although he didn't understand it, there was a vague recollection of something, deep down inside him that was troubling him as he sat waiting for what would happen next.

'You're very quiet, Emperor, are you finally seeing the danger here?' the stranger asked.

'I just want this to be finished,' he replied, barely able to respond to his captor anymore. His hopes of being saved were fading fast.

'As do I, Emperor, and I'm growing tired of waiting now. I think it's time to show yourself and others just how serious I am.' He carefully scanned the crowd around him whilst talking, plotting his next move.

'Time is running out now, so I demand that the people of Orgent bring forward their children and sit them before me,' he bellowed out to the crowd.

There was a murmuring amongst the people, but no one moved until the stranger spoke again.

'Now!' he screamed across the courtyard, and slowly people started leading their children towards him, heads bowed, knowing they had no choice.

The emperor sat watching as the large group of children were sat by the steps of the temple, some quietly sobbing to themselves, whilst others were just nervously awaiting their fate.

The evil being swept his hand across the courtyard, using his powers to drag a few men out of the shadows, forcing them to stand before him. 'Where are your children?' he asked them coldly.

'I don't have any children,' one of the men replied, avoiding eye contact and shuffling nervously before the evil intruder.

'I'm sure you'll all say the same,' the evil stranger replied, before dragging the man's son out into the open, and slashing his face with a point of his finger.

'No, stop!' the man shouted. 'Please don't hurt him — it's not his fault.'

'I know that,' said the evil being, 'it's yours.' He used his magic to start to choke the life out of the man in front of the others.

The boy cried out as he watched his father's body drop to the ground, lifeless, and rushed over to him. He began pulling on his arm, desperate for any reaction.

'Go to the others, child, before you suffer the same fate.' He moved towards the boy menacingly and the boy let go of his father's arm and ran to the others, still crying out in pain.

'The rest of you will bring your children to me now, or I'll kill you and then them.' As soon as the words were spoken, the men rushed back to the shadows and shepherded their children over to him, to join the others.

With the stranger distracted, the emperor took his chance to try to attack one of the ghostly figures guarding his people. He lunged towards one, reaching for the guard's neck, but instead found himself falling through the smoky figure and landing on the floor in a heap once more.

'You just don't understand it, do you, Emperor? You cannot fight me or my guards. We are one supreme being, and you have no power to concern us.' He mocked the emperor as he got back to his feet.

'Then kill us all and be done with it. We have nothing left,' the emperor said, defeated and close to tears.

'I gave you your chance, Emperor. Now I want the others who are bound to come here before too long. I will kill them, seize all the power and a physical form, then those here that I don't have use for, I will kill.'

'These are just children though,' the emperor argued. 'They are of no use to you.'

'They are the future of Orgent, *my* Orgent, and only I will decide what use they are. I don't need to kill them — there are plenty of adults here for that pleasure.' He cackled to himself, still growing in power with every life he took.

As the emperor slumped back to the floor again, he saw movement out of the corner of his eye, and looked up to see Elspeth appearing to float towards the dark power. Her face looked hollow and pale, but her eyes were still burning a bright red. The emperor feared they would never get her back out of the clutches of evil again, if she even survived that long.

'My Lord, I feel it has worked. She is coming, but not alone,' Elspeth said.

'Are you sure, child? I am tired of waiting and all these games. You wouldn't be lying to me, would you?'

Elspeth felt her throat tighten and she struggled to breathe, managing to whisper out a reply, 'No, my Lord, I promise you, she is on her way and will arrive soon.'

'Then I shall wait for her arrival,' he said, releasing her from his power, and turning to the emperor. 'Not long now, Emperor, and your suffering will be over.'

'Not Amelia, please, not her...'

'She will be here soon enough, Emperor, maybe I should make her my queen instead of that servant girl. What do you think? Whatever I decide, I will make sure you see it all, don't you worry.' His dark cackle filled the cold air of Orgent once more, and all the people could do was wait and see what fate had in store for them.

CHAPTER 33

On the other side of the river, the group had been making the long trek up the path towards Orgent. From the bottom of the hill, they could see the dark cloud hanging over the city, a huge contrast to the afternoon sunlight that illuminated the area around them.

None of the group were talking as they made their way towards the great walled city, too busy focusing on getting to their next destination, and what they would all be facing when they eventually arrived.

By the time the sky had started to darken, they had reached the halfway point to Orgent and Grey Moon stopped them all from going further.

'We will rest here a while, under the cover of the forest, until the others come and meet us,' he said, setting his sack down and gathering any wood he could find around them.

'When will we eat?' asked Lone Wolf, starting to feel hungry and tired.

'Soon, my friend, when the others arrive,' Grey Moon replied, heaping the wood together and starting a campfire for them to sit round whilst they waited.

The mood was strange amongst the group as they sat and waited. Tallulah was bored and poking around in the fire, whilst Black Wolf and Amelia sat huddled together close. Lone Wolf was sharpening his knife and trying not to think about food, whilst Grey Moon was staring silently into the flames.

After a while, Black Wolf jumped to his feet, noticing a fiery light appear in the woods, across the path from them. This light was soon followed by another, and then many more, practically igniting the forest beyond them. 'What is that, Grey Moon?' he said, pointing towards the lights.

'These are our people, Black Wolf. Though I should say *your* people,' he said, smiling. He got to his feet.

Across the clearing, the group watched as almost a hundred tribesmen stepped out into the open, all carrying fiery torches and weapons. Grey Moon walked over and spoke to the group, whilst the others looked on in awe, amazed by the sheer number of people who had come to fight for them.

'Step forward, Black Wolf, your people are here to greet you,' Grey Moon announced, and Black Wolf slowly walked over to join the tribesmen.

Grey Moon stood before Black Wolf and held his hand up in front of him. 'From the power given to me by our Great Mother, I give my blood back to the land, and call upon our brother, Black Wolf, to lead this tribe and our people to a new future.' Grey Moon cut his hand, wiped the blood on the ground between them and signalled for Black Wolf to hold his hand out too.

'I give my blood back to our land and thank our Great Mother for giving me the honour of ruling my people,' Black Wolf said, as he too cut his hand, following Grey Moon's lead in rubbing his blood into the dirt.

'To Black Wolf, the leader of man,' the tribe said in unison, all bowing before him.

'Your fate is nearly complete now, my child. Lead our people with strength, pride and grace and they will serve you until the end of time.' Grey Moon bowed to Black Wolf, then spoke quietly in his ear. 'They are yours to lead now, my child.' He walked back to the others.

'Thank you all,' said Black Wolf. 'I hope you brought some food with you?' As some of the tribesmen revealed large sacks full of food, he smiled and led them over to the others. 'Before we sit for food, I need to introduce you to your new leader in battle, Lone Wolf,' Black Wolf announced, taking his friend by surprise.

Lone Wolf got to his feet and bowed to the men. 'Thank you, Black Wolf — and greetings, men. Together we will rid Orgent and all our lands of this evil, letting us return to the peace that we have been accustomed to for a long time now.'

The tribesmen shouted out a battle cry, loud and as one, before bowing again. 'Now, let us eat,' said Black Wolf, and the tribesmen joined the travellers in sitting near the fire and cooking their food.

Whilst they ate, Amelia found Grey Moon sitting quietly, working with more of his herbs and pastes. 'Sorry to disturb you, Grey Moon,' she said, 'but I'm worried that time is running out for my people. Shouldn't we be there by now?'

'I understand your fears, Princess, and if you let me, I can perform a rite that will answer these fears for you. All I need is a drop of your blood.'

'Anything you need,' she replied, cutting her finger with his knife and squeezing some of her blood into a bowl, with a mixture of his herbs and spices he'd already prepared.

'Thank you, Princess.' He held the bowl over the fire until the contents started to bubble, and then steam rose from it. Slowly, he closed his eyes and inhaled the steam, letting his mind see Orgent as if he was floating above it. 'They are expecting us and are waiting. He grows stronger, but impatient. Your father and Elspeth are alive, but tomorrow we must attack,' he mumbled, as if talking in his sleep, and then he returned, his eyes open wide.

'Thank you, Grey Moon,' she said, taking his hand in hers.

'I'm not leading my men from here,' said Black Wolf, arriving out of the dark and interrupting them. 'I promised you we'd save Orgent, Amelia, and we will do that at first light, but I want us closer.' He looked deep into her eyes, appearing like the warrior he was starting to become.

Grey Moon nodded to him as if reading his mind and started to perform another ritual, burning different herbs and chanting quietly to himself.

'We need to pack up, men; we have a walk ahead of us before we rest for the night. Follow me,' Black Wolf announced to the tribesmen, who all started gathering their supplies together. 'Lone Wolf, you lead the men but keep Amelia and Tallulah by your side at all times.'

'I will, Black Wolf,' Lone Wolf replied proudly, and before long, the army made its way to Orgent with Lone Wolf, Black Wolf and Grey Moon walking on separately ahead, their fiery torches guiding them on their way.

'Won't this be dangerous?' Amelia called out to Grey Moon, who was walking just in front of her. 'Won't they see us coming?'

'Don't worry, Princess, I have one or two tricks left, trust me,' he replied. He then looked towards Black Wolf, a tear in his eye. 'You are a true leader, my child.'

And slowly the lights made their way up the path, heading to save Orgent.

CHAPTER 34

The group had made camp a short walk away from the gates of Orgent, tucked into the edge of the forest. On the journey, Black Wolf had discussed his own fears with Grey Moon about being seen before they had a chance to attack, but Grey Moon had assured him that the last ritual he'd performed would keep them invisible from the evil — if they stayed in the Great Mother's woods.

Satisfied that he wasn't leading all of them to an immediate death, Black Wolf had found a spacious area in the forest nearby, where they could be concealed by the trees but have enough room to plan their next move. In typical tribesman style, they had already lit a few small fires and were cooking more food, whilst the original group of travellers were sat together.

Black Wolf watched across the fire as Amelia and Tallulah chatted with each other, laughing and joking like a proper family. Although it was lovely to see them so close, there was still a heaviness in Black Wolf's heart that he couldn't seem to shake.

'Are you okay, my child?' Grey Moon said to him quietly.

'I don't know, Grey Moon. I'm really struggling to come to terms with how I feel about everything. It seems like another age that we were sat in our home talking about dreams, and now these people are here, different but alive, in my world. I have all these feelings but I'm confused; that was then and I don't know what to do about now.' Black Wolf's mind was racing whenever he thought about it, but it felt good to talk to his wise friend.

'You've had an awful lot to discover and work through, my child. The only thing I can say to you is that the links to the past are important, but it's what you want in *this* life that matters. Tallulah will always look up to you as a father figure, but in this life she isn't your child. You can make a different sort of life with her; it will happen naturally, given time.' Grey Moon put his hand on Black Wolf's shoulder to offer him some comfort.

'What about Amelia though?' he asked, watching her smile as she spoke to Lone Wolf.

Grey Moon smiled broadly as he spoke. 'Aaahh, the

princess, now that is different, my child. Forget the past and live now. I may be an old man, but I'm not a fool, I can see how you feel about her. Maybe once this is over you can close that chapter of the past and then you can tell her what she needs to hear. Let our Great Mother guide you, child; it will all work out as it's meant to, trust me. First you need to lead your men though.'

'Thank you, Grey Moon. You are always such a great help to me. I will make you proud, I promise,' he said, getting up and heading to the tribesmen.

'You always have, my child,' Grey Moon said wistfully to himself, rubbing the tears out of his eyes, unaware that Amelia was watching him curiously across the campfire.

'I need you to join me, Lone Wolf. We've got work to do, to get our men ready,' Black Wolf called out over his shoulder.

Lone Wolf excused himself from the group and went to join his friend. 'I didn't get a chance to tell you earlier, but thank you for giving me such an important part in your tribe. It means a lot to me.'

'You are the perfect man for the job, Lone Wolf,' Black Wolf replied. 'We need to get these men into an order where they'll be ready for battle, and I know you can do that.'

'We'll get them ready and this time tomorrow we can sit and feast after a hard-fought victory.'

'I hope so, but remember that during the battle it's your job to guard Tallulah and Amelia. Let the other men wage the war; you three are the most important.'

'What if I let you down though?' Lone Wolf said, still worrying about his place in all this.

'You won't, warrior. I have faith in you,' Black Wolf said, patting his friend on the back.

As they reached the tribesmen, they expected to find them either eating or resting. Instead, they were already practising for battle and getting weapons ready. As Black Wolf watched quietly from the cover of the trees, he turned to Lone Wolf and spoke. 'This might be easier than we thought.'

After a long time planning strategies and practising their fighting with weapons, the tribesmen were eventually allowed back to their camp, to rest for the night. Black Wolf had been impressed by their abilities and the way that Lone

Wolf had taken control of them.

'I'm going to get some rest now, Black Wolf. Thank you for your help. Tallulah can come and sleep near me if she wishes and I can guard her. Just tell her to come and find me; I will save a space for her.'

'I will, Lone Wolf. Sleep well and I'll see you in the morning,' Black Wolf said, heading back to the campfire.

When he got back, none of the others were there, so he got his book out of his sack and started to write down everything he had witnessed in his voyages into the night world since he'd last written.

'What are you writing, Black Wolf?' Amelia said, returning to the fire and sitting next to him.

'Grey Moon gave me this book before all this started and told me to write down all my dreams and visions...'

'I'd like to read it someday, if you don't mind? It'd be interesting to learn more about our old life.' She didn't want to pry into Black Wolf's privacy, but was curious to know as much as she could about their history.

'You can read it if you like, Amelia, but they are no more than campfire stories. It's now that matters,' he said, smiling at her.

'Well, you'd better not take too long writing and come and join me then,' she replied. 'I'm going to lie down and would enjoy your company when you are finished.' Then she kissed him on the cheek and headed off to settle down for the night.

'I'll be there soon,' he called, watching her walk away.

'That is the smile of a soul full of all things good,' said Grey Moon out of nowhere, as he joined his friend at the fire.

'Hello, Grey Moon. I wondered where you'd gone.'

'Not far, my child. I just walked Tallulah over to Lone Wolf's camp for the night; I knew you'd want her safe and secure. How are you?' he asked, sounding concerned.

'I'm worried about what will happen when we reach Orgent. I've become the leader of our people so quickly — what if I'm not good enough?'

'You must have faith, my child. I told you back at camp, when we started on this journey, that this was your destiny. I told you once you had learnt more about your path, then you would stand at the head of our people with great power.

This prophecy is slowly coming true, and you will lead us like no other. I believe in you.'

'I will try, Grey Moon,' Black Wolf replied doubtfully.

'What else is really troubling you?'

'I don't know. I just feel like something is missing but I cannot understand what. I've been writing my dreams down like you said, but there are still pieces that don't make sense to me. It's like I cannot see everything yet.'

'That's natural, my child. Your journey has only just begun in some ways. You still have lots to discover, but you will. That is all for another time.' Grey Moon put his hand on Black Wolf's shoulder and a strange spark ignited in both of them. Grey Moon quickly stood up and started to walk away, saying, 'I must rest now and so should you. It will be a long day tomorrow. Goodnight, my child.'

Black Wolf sat by the fire a little longer, thinking, before he too got up and went to join Amelia. All the time his mind was working hard, trying to fill in the missing pieces. He knew he needed rest; tomorrow would be hard. However, as he lay down, curling himself around Amelia, he kept thinking of the spark he received when Grey Moon had touched him.

As he drifted off to sleep he wanted to know why he'd seen the tree stump again, only this time he recognised the stranger with the kind face. It was Grey Moon.

CHAPTER 35

Everything was eerily quiet behind the temple's doors. Majila and Kaliam had been walking down corridors for a long time, but there was no sign of life. Although the temple looked big from the outside, it was even bigger within the confines of the great white walls.

Eventually they reached an area where the corridor widened and rooms branched off from both sides of the walls. As they walked along, they looked into the separate rooms; each had a beautifully carved door that was wide open and inside they could see all the riches of the palace decorating the walls, with huge woven rugs and cushions on the floor. Majila was taken aback by the beauty of the rooms, but his hopes were fading fast at finding Esmee; all of these rooms were completely empty.

Kaliam spoke as if reading Majila's mind. 'These are the rooms for prayers and teaching the children. The largest is at the end of this passageway, it's not that far.'

They carried on searching until the corridor turned a sharp corner; when they reached it Kaliam held his hand up, motioning for them to stop, and signalled that they needed to speak quietly.

'Around this corner is a small walkway and the largest room that I mentioned,' he whispered, before crouching close to the floor and sliding his sword slowly past the edge of the wall. Majila crouched next to him and together they looked at the blade that reflected the view from down the hallway.

In the reflection, they could see one guard stood at the doorway, facing down towards them. He was standing still, like the others had been, holding his sword across his chest, standing guard over the room. Beyond him, the door was open and they could just make out a large amount of children all sat cross-legged on the floor. They were all silent, but Majila could see from some of the reflected faces that this was out of fear.

'I have a plan, my friend,' Kaliam whispered to Majila before carefully pulling his sword back. 'It'll be safer if I distract him. They know you, but I am just another of the city's inhabitants. Be ready to act when the guard moves.'

He stepped back and then walked round the corner, in the opposite direction of the guard.

Majila heard a shout but waited, pressed against the wall, until the guard hurried by, in pursuit of Kaliam. Pulling his sword out from its sheath, Majila bounded forward, silently grabbing the guard and slitting his throat from behind. The blood spurted and flew at the wall, painting a wide arc of crimson against the pure white stone, his body slamming loudly to the floor. Kaliam walked back from the doorway he was headed for and joined Majila, kicking the guard's body out of his way after taking his sword.

'Well done, my friend. That was easier than I thought. We must move now though; we need to find Esmee.'

Together they ran along the hallway and entered the room. It was full of children, all sitting silently; they didn't appear hurt but they were all terrified. Majila scanned the faces in front of him, then he froze as the realisation hit him: Esmee was nowhere to be seen.

'Esmee's not here, Kaliam! All the children seem to be here but she's not. It's too late, they must have got her.' Majila was beside himself with worry and Kaliam had to grab him by the shoulders, holding him firmly until he appeared to calm.

'Then we carry on further and keep searching until we find her. Do not give up hope — maybe she escaped? If she is still in the temple then we will find her, you have my word.'

Kaliam moved past Majila, starting to head towards the door at the end of the hallway. Majila stopped him by putting his arm in front of him, and Kaliam noticed the intensity in his friend's eyes.

'This is my battle now, my friend,' Majila said. 'You have done enough. I will find Esmee, but I need you to get these children out of here and find them safety. I cannot have anyone else die in my name, so please take them and go.'

Kaliam could see that there was no point in arguing with Majila, no matter how much he wanted to stay by his side. He looked back at the faces of the children and knew his friend was right. He looked Majila in the eyes as he spoke, matching his friend's intensity. 'I will get the children to safety and then I will come back for you. I won't let you do this alone.'

'That door leads to a balcony. Follow it to the end you'll

find one last set of steps leading up to the main temple room. That is the only place we haven't searched. I will take the children out and down the steps to safety, then I will return to you there.' Kaliam started to herd the children back down the long hallway they had searched along earlier. Once all the children were moving, he followed behind them, speaking to Majila one last time. 'You are a true warrior, Majila. Somehow, I fear for your enemies more than I do for you. That fire inside you, may it burn eternally. I will see you again soon, my friend.' Kaliam bowed his head to Majila before walking away, after the children.

'I won't forget you, Kaliam,' was all Majila said before heading out through the door and onto the balcony. The cold air hitting him was a huge contrast to the warmth inside the temple walls. He smiled as he took one last look back at his friend leading the children to safety, but his concentration was soon brought flooding back when he heard Esmee's cry echoing further along the balcony.

Moving quickly but quietly, Majila raced along the walkway until he saw the steps Kaliam had spoken of. There were two guards visible, one stood at the bottom of the steps and the other was struggling to climb them. As he watched, he saw the guard was struggling because he was pulling Esmee along with him by her arms, which were tied together at the wrists. She was appearing to drag her feet and pull him back but his strength was overwhelming her, and bit by bit she was slowly being pulled up the steps.

Majila could wait no more; filled with anger, he raced at the lone guard with his sword drawn. The guard didn't hear the footsteps until it was too late and, just as he turned to look, Majila caught him across the side of his head with the heavy base of the sword's handle. The guard's legs buckled and he overbalanced, sending his flailing body over the small wall and hurtling to the stone floor far below, at the base of the temple.

The guard with Esmee reacted by pulling her harder until they reached the huge doors at the top of the steps.

'Give me my daughter and I won't harm you, you have my word.' Majila stood facing the guard, his eyes full of anger and burning like fire.

'You have no power here, native. All you have are your threats and a sword. If you want your precious daughter then come and get her.' The guard held Esmee by the throat, pulling her backwards through the doors.

Without thinking, Majila rushed up the stairs after her, crying out as he lost sight of her disappearing through the huge doors. 'Esmee!' The name echoed around the stone walls and as Majila reached the door, he felt something solid strike him heavily against the side of his head, and then everything went black.

CHAPTER 36

The loud crack of thunder and bright flash of lightning woke the group instantly. Tallulah clung to Lone Wolf, scared by the noise. Black Wolf sat up next to Amelia, alert, sensing that something was wrong.

'This is his doing,' Grey Moon said, suddenly appearing next to his friend. 'He has grown even more powerful than I imagined — we must move soon.'

Another huge crack of thunder stopped Black Wolf from replying, and then a voice boomed out around the forest where they were camped.

'I know you are out there, Princess, and I know you can hear me. My patience has worn thin with your games; come to Orgent and surrender. I'll make it very simple for you: give yourself up now, or you'll die and so will all of your people. Starting with your beloved father.' The stranger's voice was so loud that some of the tribesmen were searching the forest around them, sure that he must have been hiding nearby.

Enraged by his threat and panicking for her people, Amelia grabbed Black Wolf and pleaded with him. 'We must go now — we can stop anyone else from getting hurt, please, Black Wolf.'

'That is what he wants, Princess, trust me,' Grey Moon assured her. 'He cannot know we're here because of our Great Mother's powers. He is trying to get you to react, so then he has us all exactly where he wants us.'

'But we cannot sit here and do nothing,' she replied desperately.

'We won't,' Black Wolf said, his eyes fixated on the top of the path. 'We will keep him as blind as we can and then we will attack. If he feels we ignored his challenge he will be shocked and forced to make a new plan. That is when we will appear. Tallulah, Grey Moon, didn't you say about faery charm and their links to nature?'

'Yes, Black Wolf, that is true,' replied Grey Moon.

'Then make it rain; we need the cover.'

Tallulah and Grey Moon sat down by the campfire and performed a ritual, which mixed his native traditions and her faery rites, whilst the others watched quietly. As another shard of lighting cut across the sky above Orgent, the rain started to fall, slowly at first, and then it started to pour down from the sky.

'Men, follow my lead,' Black Wolf ordered, and he used the wet mud around them, painting his cheeks and his forehead first, and then his arms. 'You said the magic would work if we stayed under cover of nature didn't you, Grey Moon?' he asked.

'Yes...' answered Grey Moon, slightly confused.

'Earth is the heart of our Great Mother's land; there is no purer form of nature.'

'I hadn't thought of that,' Grey Moon replied, smiling. 'Yes, you are right. That will get you to the city without being seen.'

'Won't the rain wash the mud away and leave us visible?' Amelia asked.

'It doesn't matter, Amelia. We'll already be there.'

'He needs to see the princess coming alone. That will create a bigger distraction for you,' Grey Moon said.

'No, it's too dangerous,' Black Wolf replied. 'I won't put her in danger.'

'They already know I'm coming,' Amelia said firmly. 'Grey Moon told me so with his vision — and they're my people. I want to do this.'

Black Wolf cupped his hands around her face as he spoke, 'They took you once, and I cannot risk them taking you again.'

'It's fine, Black Wolf, trust me. This is how I want it to be. I will be fine — I have you to protect me.'

'The princess is right, Black Wolf. This is how it must be,' Grey Moon agreed, and Black Wolf realised that he would have to let her have her way.

'Men, cover yourselves. We follow the princess. You all know the plan, you practised and showed me your skills, now show me your courage,' he announced to the group, who were already covering themselves in the mud. 'You too, Tallulah,' he added, and watched as she did as he asked without any argument.

Together they walked the last bit of their journey up the path to the huge wooden doors of Orgent. Amelia was in front, carrying a flaming torch, with Grey Moon, Black Wolf and Tallulah behind, followed by Lone Wolf and his army.

When they reached the doors, they could feel the chill

emanating from within. The army were crouched low as Amelia walked towards the huge wooden doors. Grey Moon was beside her, and spilt a mixture of dry powder out of bags along the bottom of the doors, before retreating into the darkness nearby.

'Drop your torch, Princess,' he whispered from the shadows, and she did.

They all watched as a few seconds later the doors caught alight, and within minutes the two doors were burning furiously, the sound of crackling wood filling the dark, cold air. In the shadows, the men watched the fire raging, and silently waited.

CHAPTER 37

They hadn't been waiting outside Orgent long when they heard a loud creaking and they watched as the huge burning doors slowly opened before them.

'It's time, Amelia,' Black Wolf said.

Slowly, Amelia stepped through the thick smoke and into the courtyard of Orgent. As she did so she scanned the area, making out all the people cowering in their doorways, and she came to a stop just inside the gates.

'Welcome home, Princess. I've been waiting for you.'

Amelia stood still, desperately trying to keep calm and not show how scared she was. She watched the huge, cloaked figure glide across the floor towards her. Behind him, she saw her father looking up at her from the floor, his eyes wide in fright.

'You wanted me and here I am — now let my father and the others go,' she demanded with false bravado.

'You're welcome to him,' the stranger scoffed, using his powers to send the emperor flying across the floor, dumping him at her feet.

'Father, are you hurt?' she asked, fighting back the tears as she bent down to him. 'I'm so sorry, I should never have left you.'

'It's not your fault, my child,' said the emperor.

'Leaving was your best idea, Princess,' the evil being interrupted. 'The mistake you made was returning, now there is no hope for you. You are alone, and powerless to stop me.'

'I am many things,' she spat angrily at him, 'but I am not alone.'

Slowly, Black Wolf stepped out of the smoke behind her. He was followed by Tallulah and Lone Wolf, and they all stood at Amelia's side, showing a united front.

'Oh, you have friends. How nice,' the stranger said mockingly. 'So these are the visitors your beloved Elspeth told me about?'

'Where is Elspeth?' Amelia replied, feeling a cold chill run down her spine.

Amelia watched as Elspeth appeared from behind the stranger, again seemingly floating across the floor. Her eyes were burning red and she looked pale and thin. The bloodied cut on her cheek made her appear even more frightening. She came to a halt next to the stranger.

'Here is your beloved servant, Princess. Although I imagine she's not quite what you expected to find. I'm afraid she's not feeling herself at the minute.' The stranger cackled to himself.

'What have you done to her?' Amelia shouted at him, but as she stepped forward to hold her friend, Black Wolf grabbed her arm. 'Leave her, Amelia. She's a part of him now — the Elspeth you know is gone. I'm sorry.'

'You will pay for this, I promise you,' she spat at the stranger, the emotion catching in her throat.

'Who will make me pay, Princess? The four of you, with sticks and stones?' he replied, as Elspeth laughed eerily.

'I have had enough of this. Give the city back to the people now, or suffer a worse fate than you could ever give to them,' Lone Wolf said, stepping forward defiantly.

'Really? You think you can rid the city of me, do you? Four simple souls, facing a power of which they know nothing,' he said, his red eyes burning into his opponent's.

Suddenly, Lone Wolf let out an almost animalistic cry, and the stranger watched as a huge number of tribesmen came flooding into Orgent, through the flaming doorway.

'I think we stand a good chance,' said Lone Wolf proudly, as his men took up a formation behind them, ready to attack when needed.

'Lots of men, I see, but no power,' said the evil being, sending his black smoke out towards the remaining guards he had captured when taking Orgent, and the group watched as they all started choking on the smoke that was flooding into them.

'I can gather men, it's not a problem for me,' he said. 'Guards, stand ready.' And the guards moved forward until they were standing before the dark power, their eyes now as red as his, staring blankly at the group.

'This is his power — you don't stand a chance,' the emperor said desperately to Amelia. 'You need to get away from here.'

'We will fight to the death, Emperor, if that is what it takes,' said Black Wolf.

'I am growing tired of these children and their silly

boasts. Guards, seize them,' ordered the dark power, and the guards stepped forwards with their swords drawn.

Outside Orgent, Grey Moon remained alone in the shadows, next to a small fire he'd lit from the burning doors. 'Great Mother, we need your help if we are to save your land. Grant me the power to conceal my plans, I beg of you.' He spoke softly, in one of his trances, and he watched as the bags of herbs he'd prepared earlier started smoking. Peering round the fiery doors, he threw the bags as far as he could along the floor of the city, in the direction of the group. The thick smoke started billowing out into the courtyard, obscuring everything, and it provided perfect cover for the group as the guards prepared to seize them.

'Now!' shouted Lone Wolf and the first line of his tribesmen went to war with the guards. Their native weapons didn't have much of an impact, but enabled them to at least hold their own against the guards' swords.

'We won't be able to hold out for long, unless you can make it to the armoury!' Amelia said to Black Wolf as the group crouched down, hidden by Grey Moon's smoke.

'Take me and we'll get in there safely. I can use my powers of charm if anyone tries to attack us,' said Tallulah, fighting her fears.

'It's your only chance,' Amelia said before Black Wolf could argue.

'I'll take her and some men, then we'll return,' said Lone Wolf.

'Okay, but be quick — and if it's too dangerous then come straight back and we'll have to work out another plan,' Black Wolf ordered. 'I won't lose you.'

Tallulah picked up two of the smoking bags and threw a third in the direction Amelia had shown to them. Then, with Lone Wolf and a handful of tribesmen, they headed to get some stronger weapons.

The smoke from Grey Moon, combined with that of the dark power, had caused chaos in the centre of the courtyard. The guards and tribesmen were still exchanging blows as the stranger waited patiently for his next move. Amelia and Black Wolf stayed together by the emperor, with a few more tribesmen stood guarding them from any attack.

The evil being's voice echoed loudly around the courtyard as the battle raged on. 'What a fantastic show.'

CHAPTER 38

As the weapons clashed around Orgent, neither side were gaining any advantage. The tribesmen fought bravely but, without equal weapons, all they could really do was defend themselves without being able to launch a proper attack.

Keeping tight against Orgent's wall, Tallulah, Lone Wolf and the tribesmen were making their way into the armoury at the guards' main quarters. Tallulah had used one of the smoking bags to conceal them as they crept carefully along, but the fighting in the centre of the courtyard also provided a huge distraction for them and they made it safely to their destination without being detected.

In the armoury was a vast array of unfinished weapons and old ones that were far too damaged to be of any use anymore, but on the back wall of the room was a large collection of swords that were ready and waiting for the guards.

'Men, take at least three swords each if you can and then we need to get back to the princess,' Lone Wolf ordered, picking up a sword at random. It felt strangely familiar to him but he didn't have time to find out why.

'There isn't much smoke left in this bag,' Tallulah said. 'We'd better go now; I'm not sure my charm alone is enough to protect us.'

The men gathered as many swords as they could carry, and under the cover of the last smoke bag they headed back to join the others. On their journey, Lone Wolf looked at Tallulah and remembered exactly why that sword was familiar to him.

'You're being so brave, Tallulah. I won't let anything happen to you,' he said, thoughts of the sword taking him back to the past and his job of protecting her previously.

'Thank you, Lone Wolf,' she replied, starting to move quicker as the smoke began to thin and disappear.

In the centre of the courtyard, the tribesmen had increased in numbers and were starting to force the guards to retreat. Seeing this, Lone Wolf gave an order to the men with him. 'We are nearly back with the princess. Take the weapons and join them in battle — this is our best chance!'

The tribesmen ran over to the others, and swords were

exchanged during battle, enabling all the tribesmen to put up an even greater fight. Sensing that the battle was starting to turn against him, the evil intruder sent an order to his ghostly men and they came away from the city's inhabitants and joined the fight.

When Lone Wolf and Tallulah made it back to the others the swords were clashing noisily in the cold night air. Both the evil stranger and Black Wolf's group had moved further back as the space between them filled with more and more fighting men. Orgent's guards were losing ground and the bloodied bodies were falling in large numbers around them, littering the courtyard and filling the air with the sickly smell of blood.

'These are men I grew up with… They protected me,' Amelia said to Black Wolf, tears welling in her eyes as she watched the guards.

'I know, Amelia, but they aren't those people anymore. They are already lost to the evil and we cannot get them back. There is only one way to help them now,' he replied, pulling her towards him and shielding her from all the bloodshed.

As the last of the guards fell, the ghostly figures moved in closer to the tribesmen. They had no weapons other than their power, but the group knew that this was dangerous enough and could cause endless amounts of horror in an attempt to defeat their opponents.

'I can't just sit here and watch our men fight, I should be out there with them,' Lone Wolf said to Black Wolf.

'Keep calm, Lone Wolf. Your time will come, but for now just let them fight. You need to protect Tallulah.'

'They don't stand a chance — we are already defeated,' the emperor said, his head hanging low again. 'Just watch.'

The group watched as the tribesmen sliced through the oncoming wave of ghostly figures, but no sooner did the swords plunge through them, than they multiplied. Before everyone's eyes, one ghostly figure became two, two became four, and on it went. With each blow landed, the ghostly figures appeared to become weaker, but the growing number made it even harder for the tribesmen to cope

'You will fall before too long and your city will become mine, Princess,' the evil being called coldly across the bloody courtyard floor.

'Never!' screamed Amelia, a mixture of grief and rage.

As Grey Moon's smoke finally started to run out and dissipate in the air, the group saw the full extent of the horrors before them. All of the remaining guards had been killed — but so had many of the tribesmen. Bodies littered the centre of Orgent and the tribesmen were starting to retreat, fearing the immense power that they were facing.

CHAPTER 39

'Keep fighting, men! They might be growing in number, but they are getting weaker,' Lone Wolf ordered. After retreating to recoup for a while, the tribe surged forward again, screaming at their opponents as they ran forward, waving their swords in the air.

The evil being could feel his own power waning as his ghostly army used it to keep multiplying when they were attacked; he knew he had to do something to gain some extra strength.

'Your time has come, servant girl. The princess is here so I have no use for you anymore,' The evil stranger reached towards Elspeth, making a grabbing action in mid-air, pulling his magic back out of her and putting it back into himself. Already feeling the strength starting to build up inside himself again, he turned to Amelia and spoke, 'Take your servant girl back, Princess. She is of no use to me anymore.'

Dazed, Elspeth staggered away from the evil being, towards Amelia. Her eyes had returned to her normal colour but she had blood coming from her nose and mouth.

'Princess, help me, please,' she said weakly, before dropping face first to the floor.

'Elspeth!' Amelia cried and broke free from Black Wolf, running over to her friend's body and pulling her back to where the emperor was sitting.

'I'm sorry, Princess, I didn't want to help him but I couldn't fight his power.' The girl sobbed quietly to herself, all the strength slowly draining from her body, as the blood continued to flow down her face.

'Shh, Elspeth, it's okay. Just hold on and we'll get you out of here,' the princess said, fighting back tears.

'I'm so tired... I just want to sleep.' Elspeth's voice was barely a whisper, and then her head slumped onto Amelia's chest.

'No, Elspeth, no! Wake up, please just wake up!' Amelia sobbed, rocking backwards and forwards with her friend's lifeless body held tightly in her arms. 'Why her? She was innocent! She has nothing to do with this!' she screamed at the evil intruder, who laughed.

'You're right, Princess, she was nothing. Especially now!'

Amelia tried to get to her feet, but Black Wolf stopped her, his hands on her shoulders as he spoke softly in her ear, 'He wants you to go to him, Amelia. Don't be fooled by him.' And then he turned to Lone Wolf. 'Whatever happens, you keep them here with you, safe.'

The dark power was stronger but still needed to gain more magic if he was to succeed. Slowly, he used his power to grab one of the fighting tribesmen and hung him in the air between the fighters.

Slowly the ghostly figures disappeared, one by one, and the remaining tribesmen fell through fresh air and landed in heaps on the floor with no opponents left to fight. When they realised this, they stood to face the dark power and instead watched as one of their own people was choked to death in mid-air and the body was discarded on the city floor, by their feet.

'You cannot defeat me, Princess. I will use all your men and just get stronger. I haven't even started with the fire yet. You remember the fire don't you, Black Wolf?' He laughed coldly to himself again.

Black Wolf couldn't listen to any more and launched himself at the evil being, wild with anger.

'Black Wolf, no!' shouted Amelia, but it was too late; the evil being caught his body as it leapt towards him, then sent it flying towards the city gates. Black Wolf's head connected with the wall and he fell to the floor, unconscious, whilst Amelia looked on, her mouth and eyes wide with fright.

CHAPTER 40

The freezing cold water woke Majila from his slumber. His head was pounding and he was struggling to clear his vision. He leant forward to rub his eyes and realised his hands were tied tightly to the chair behind his back; panicking, he tried to move his legs and found they too were tightly bound, at the ankles. He struggled against the ropes to try to free himself but they wouldn't loosen. The chair edged slightly across the stone floor but he was completely trapped.

'You cannot escape, Majila, it is pointless trying. Even if you broke free from your ties, you wouldn't make it out of this room alive.' A loud voice cut through the fog of Majila's thoughts, bringing him back to the feeling of dread that waking up in this room had given him.

Slowly his sight started to clear and he could see what was facing him. He was in a large room that had no windows and it was empty except for two guards stood to his side and one huge figure in front of him.

The figure signalled to the guards and they dumped something on the floor between Majila and himself. Majila looked horrified as he saw a mop of blonde hair fall from beneath the blanket on the floor and he realised it was Esmee.

'What have you done to her? If you've hurt her, I swear I will kill all of you.' Majila was snarling as he spat his words towards the shadowy figure stood before him.

The stranger stepped forward and pulled back the blanket, revealing a dazed Esmee laying on the floor. Majila carried on struggling against the ropes, powerless to help, as he watched the stranger grab Esmee by the hair and lift her head towards him.

'I haven't hurt her yet, but I will if you force my hand. Hand yourself in now and she'll be freed. This child is of no use to me; it's you I want, Majila.' The stranger stared deep into Majila's eyes and continued to pull Esmee's head back.

Majila remained defiant whilst trying to loosen his hands from behind him. 'How do I know she'll be safe? Once you have me you could kill her too. I don't trust you, your words mean nothing to me.'

The stranger signalled to the guards and one of them

bought their sword out and held it towards him. Majila watched as the stranger placed his hands over the tip of the sword and mumbled quietly to himself. As he did so, Majila saw fire appear from nowhere between the stranger's hands, heating the tip of the sword until it glowed with a fierce heat. Then he turned to Majila and spoke.

'I am born of the darkest fire, Majila, one that holds all in eternal damnation. I can unleash it at will and take all it engulfs with me. My word may mean nothing to you, but it is always to be obeyed. You have offended me enough, so now I shall say one more time. Come with me and your daughter is free, or watch as I burn her pretty little face into your mind forever.'

The stranger held Esmee's head at an angle and the guard moved his sword towards her cheek. The air filled with the smell of burning as the blade singed bits of her hair. Majila watched as the sword got closer and knew he had no choice. Aalym's voice rang through his mind: *You must save Esmee.*

'Stop, please just stop. She is just a child! You can take me, but please don't harm her.' The tears of anger were welling up in his eyes as he spoke and he slumped in relief as the guard withdrew his sword and the stranger dropped Esmee back to the floor.

'Please, just let me say goodbye though. She is all I have left in this world.' Majila begged for a chance to hold her one last time.

The stranger nodded to the second guard and he cut the ropes that bound Majila to the chair. Majila sank to the floor, desperately crawling to Esmee and cradling her in his arms.

'My beautiful child, I am so sorry. I failed you and your mother. You are my little soul, my future, I will pray for you every day until I can find you again.' Majila sobbed as he hugged her dazed body close. Through glassy eyes she looked up at him and smiled slightly. With a curious look on her face she spoke one word, which was more of a question than a statement.

'Safe?'

She then lolled back sleepily in his arms as Majila cried into her hair.

'You see, Majila, this is your problem and that of all

mankind. Your love makes you weak. We will destroy you all and leave only the blackest of hearts in your place.' The stranger taunted Majila, his dark laugh echoing loudly around the cold stone room.

Slowly Majila stood up and faced the stranger, his body shaking with anger and the grief of all those people he had seen destroyed. With a shaky voice he attempted one last act of defiance as he faced his adversary.

'It is you who is wrong. My love makes me stronger than you could imagine. I will face you again and you will burn in your own flame for all the acts of evil you have performed. I will find you in the next life, trust me, and I will finish you.' With these words, Majila drew his hidden sword and plunged it deep into his skull, killing himself instantly, his lifeless body dropping to the floor at the stranger's feet.

The stranger let out a blood-curdling roar and, slowly, his body turned into a thick black ash that gathered on the floor and blew away under the door and out into the sky, away from the temple walls. The guards were watching in horror. Realising there was no one left to lead them, they moved towards the door to escape, just as Kaliam kicked it open.

They couldn't draw their swords quickly enough to launch any form of attack, and Kaliam sliced one across the chest before circling round and plunging his sword deep into the other guard's stomach. With the two guards dead, he moved quickly to Majila's body but realised it was too late. Blood poured from the huge wound in Majila's head and Kaliam fought back the tears as it spilled over his hands and body.

'I'm so sorry, Majila, it should have been me.' As he spoke the words aloud, Kaliam wept for the loss of his friend. He said a silent prayer and covered Majila with the blanket. As he did so, he noticed Esmee stirring next to him. Wiping his hands clean, he picked Esmee up in his arms, cradling her gently as he stood up.

'It's okay, my child, you are safe now. Keep your eyes closed and I'll get you away from here.' Esmee stirred slightly but cuddled in closely to Kaliam as he headed out the main door and back down the steps where Majila had been captured.

Kaliam ran as fast as he could, cradling Esmee in his arms the whole time, until he made it to the foot of the mountains where the other children had gone. The members of the city who had made it out safely during the attack were gathered together, planning their next move. Some of the adults had gathered things that could be used as shelter and others had food. Across the crowd of people, Kaliam caught sight of Drei Ran, walking slowly away from the group towards the city walls. He left Esmee with one of the women tending to the children and caught up with him. He grabbed him by the arm, stopping him in his tracks and glared accusingly at him.

'Where are you going? Abandoning others again are you? You're very good at that.' He spat the words in Drei Ran's direction, as he pointed towards Esmee.

Drei Ran lowered his head from Kaliam's gaze.

'No, Kaliam, I'm not leaving anyone. I tried to warn them, it wasn't safe here and I didn't want so many sacrificed. This is a great evil and we never stood a chance.'

'Then where are you going?'

Drei Ran pointed to the sky above the city.

'The city is safe now, they wanted Majila and he gave himself to save us. We can go home.' He spoke with sadness as he looked at the dark cloud above him.

Kaliam watched in shock as the cloud appeared to sift downwards in a funnel before shooting out across the plain and out of sight. Small bits of ash scattered to the ground and he realised it was the dark force moving away from them, far off into the distance.

'But what of Esmee? She is his child, surely they will come back for her?' Kaliam knew it was his duty to protect her now.

'She is just a child, they cannot sense her power until she's older. Until then we are safe, she is yours to guard though.' He headed back to the city again.

Kaliam looked back at Esmee and wept at the loss of Majila, her father and his friend. Alone, he held Majila's blood-stained knife in his hand and looked towards the sky.

'Majila, my brave friend. I will keep your child safe, I promise. Move gently into the next world and one day it will be me who gives my life for you. Until then, my friend, rest peacefully.'

Kaliam wiped away his tears and composed himself. This wasn't the time for regret; this was the time to protect Esmee.

CHAPTER 41

Black Wolf awoke minutes later, face down on the floor, his head in the shadows of Orgent's doorway. Dazed, he scrambled around, trying to clear his head, vaguely aware that someone was with him.

'Stay calm, Black Wolf, it's me. I used my medicines to bring you round. You'll feel a bit dizzy for a moment, but you'll be normal again before too long.'

Through his foggy mind, Black Wolf recognised Grey Moon's voice and sat upright.

'Where have you been, Grey Moon? Elspeth is dead and many of our tribe too. We're losing this fight — we need you!'

'It's not my time yet, my child,' he said, helping Black Wolf back to his feet. 'You need to go back and face him, but don't rush in. He has power — but so do the four of you. Let him know who he is facing.'

Then Grey Moon slipped back into the shadows, leaving Black Wolf to get back to his feet. As he slowly walked back to face the dark power, his mind was flooded with the visions he'd just seen, and he knew it was time to take revenge for everything that had been done to him in the past.

As he reached the others, he saw Amelia's face; she was sobbing as Lone Wolf held her tightly. Then he looked at Tallulah and took a deep breath before stepping back into the light again.

'Black Wolf, you're alive?' Amelia cried as he appeared.

'You should have stayed down, Black Wolf,' the evil being taunted. 'You could have saved yourself more pain and the suffering of seeing me take the lives of your loved ones for the second time.'

Black Wolf ignored the comment. 'I'm fine, Amelia. I told you I wouldn't leave you,' he said, before stepping forward in front of the group, facing the evil one on his own, with all of the tribesmen having retreated in fear.

'We came here to end this and we will,' he said defiantly. 'What you face is more than you know. You wanted the princess because she is one of the powerful ones, but what you have here are all four together. The four chosen ones, picked by our Great Mother. You are nothing more than the child she abandoned.'

The evil being looked at the four of them, silently taking stock of this new information before speaking. 'You may well be the four chosen ones, but you are all thieves who took what was rightfully mine, and I want it back. You are no threat to me anyway; you know very little of what you speak. You are nothing without the only other power I know of, the one who trapped me in this ghostly prison. You are nothing without the teacher.'

'It is you who is wrong!' a voice called out from the city gates, silencing them all, and Grey Moon walked forward with the carved wooden box in his hands. 'It has been a long time, my old friend,' he said, as the tribe and group parted, letting him walk forward to join Black Wolf.

'You are one of the powers?' Black Wolf muttered to him, surprised by this revelation.

The dark power sneered. 'You are an old man, but then you always were. Weak and pathetic, always longing to be important. Finally you think you can be, do you, Grey Moon?'

'Let's see, shall we?' Grey Moon replied, before settling the box on the floor between them, all four carved symbols glowing strongly, leaving just the eye in the middle, pale and wooden.

'Our Great Mother, now is the time of reckoning. All your children are gathered together. Let the blood I offer you illuminate our path.' Grey Moon took his knife and cut his hand, letting it drip onto the box in front of them, and they all watched as the final carving came alive in glorious colour, leaving the box and all its carvings glowing solidly.

'It *is* you,' the evil being said, sounding less confident than before. 'Then why not join me and we can rule together? You have tried to rid these lands of me before, as have many others, and you've all failed. Join me and you can free yourself from your own prison too.'

'You know I will never join you,' Grey Moon replied. 'Our Great Mother created a balance in our lands. A balance between light and dark, between right and wrong. These have and always will exist and the good must prevail. You are just one, whereas the good are many. We are a collective, born of flesh and blood, with goodness in our hearts.'

'How dare you preach to me, you and these peasants you call your people?' the evil being demanded. 'Without me in this world there is no balance, just a collection of gutless natives who see out their days breeding, hunting and carving wood. You have no greater plan, just an ancient ideal, and all that makes you is weak. Next you will be talking about love, I imagine?'

'There is no point; you know nothing of love, just greed. You kill innocence and destroy lands because you don't understand them or their ways. You feel threatened by this lack of knowledge, scared even, and when we speak of love it means nothing to you. Even your own mother didn't love you enough to let you live the way you wanted to because she saw that it was wrong. You are the child she regrets,' Grey Moon said, every word hitting the dark power hard.

'Enough!' screamed the evil being. His eyes burned darker as his anger consumed him.

'Why else would she want me to put you in your prison? I gave up my own life to stop you from destroying all our lands, but it was at her request. You fear us and that is why you rely on trickery to try to rule the land. It is time to end this now and send you back to the world of the dead souls, where she wanted you to be.'

'I'll see you there first!' the evil being screamed in anger and flung his arms out towards Grey Moon, sending a bolt of fiery energy directly into his chest. The force of the blow took him off of his feet and crashing to the ground, his body twitching, as the dark power prepared to finish his old foe, once and for all.

CHAPTER 42

Black Wolf dropped to his knees, gently lifting Grey Moon's head, desperate to get a response from him. His body was still twitching slightly but his eyes were open and he seemed aware of his surroundings.

'Get the men to cover us until he's able to stand again,' he ordered Lone Wolf, who signalled to the remaining tribesmen for them to step in front of the group again.

The evil being had his hand held out in front of him and they could all see the energy sparking in the palm of his hand, as he prepared to launch another attack on his opponent.

'I can see you have your hands full; it's fine, I can wait. Let me know when you are ready to finish our fight, Grey Moon,' the evil being goaded Grey Moon, as he continued to display his power to the watching group.

'Grey Moon, speak to me. It's me, Black Wolf, can you hear me?'

'I can hear you, my child,' Grey Moon replied, wincing with pain, the twitching starting to subside.

'How badly hurt are you? What can I do?' Black Wolf was desperate to help his friend.

'It's bad, my child, but I'll be fine. I need you to help me get to my feet though, I need to face him.' Grey Moon started to get up and Black Wolf put his arms under his friend's, helping him to stand.

Once more, the group parted for Grey Moon to face the dark power, only this time he was being held up by Black Wolf. When he reached his opponent, Grey Moon struggled forward alone, 'It is okay, my child, I need to do this myself,' he said softly to Black Wolf.

'You are a fool, old teacher. You should have stayed down — it was your only hope of surviving. Now I'll have to finish you...' The vile being sighed to himself, starting to build his power up again.

'I have an offering for you. Please, hear me out,' Grey Moon said. 'Let these people go and take me instead. You are right, I am old, and am tired of the fight now. So take me and my power but let those here go free.'

'No, Grey Moon. What are you saying?' Black Wolf

shouted at his friend in shock. 'You cannot do this, he'll kill us all anyway. You cannot surrender to him.'

'He is right, Black Wolf. We have no choice, this is for the best. I will be under his command, and you can all walk free,' Grey Moon said, his eyes glancing down to the knife on his belt.

'At last you speak sense, old man. Come join with me then and let all the lands be ours,' the dark power ordered.

'No, Grey Moon, please,' Black Wolf said, fearing for his friend and reaching out to stop him.

'Get your hands off me, child. I have made my choice and I will join this great power so that together we can rule,' Grey Moon said. 'Master, let me come and bow before you as a sign of my loyalty.'

'Yes, old teacher, you may,' the evil being replied smugly.

With the group watching on, Grey Moon walked towards the evil one, slowly slipping his knife from his belt and concealing it in the sleeve of his robe. When he reached the dark-cloaked figure, he got down on one knee and spoke, 'Allow me to serve you, master, as you become the emperor of this land and all others around it.'

'Good. You may stand now,' the evil being said.

Sensing a perfect opportunity, Grey Moon slipped the handle of the knife into the palm of his hand. He stood and leapt forward, aiming to pierce the vile being in the chest. The evil one saw the blade and stepped back quickly, before sending another bolt of energy in Grey Moon's body. The bolt hit Grey Moon in the chest again, and this time the smell of burnt flesh permeated the air as his body fell backwards into Black Wolf's outstretched arms.

'How dare you try to defy me!' roared the evil being, reeling backwards; the energy he'd conjured up seemed to sap him of some strength.

Black Wolf looked at his friend, helpless in his arms. His cloak was charred where the energy had hit him and Black Wolf removed it, folding it up behind his head as he rested him gently on the floor.

'I'm sorry, my child,' Grey Moon stammered breathlessly. 'I thought it would work. I've let you all down.'

Black Wolf fought the emotions that were building up inside him. 'Don't say that, Grey Moon, you are a brave warrior. It isn't your fault, believe me. Your wound looks bad though. How can I fix it?'

'I don't think you can, my child. Leave me and save the others — it's too late.'

'I won't lose you,' Black Wolf said firmly and he dragged his friend back to the shadows of Orgent's doorway, where he had been helped by him earlier. He found Grey Moon's sack and took out a mixture of paste that they had used to heal Amelia's wounds when they first met her, and the herbs he'd been woken with. 'Amelia, quick, come help me,' he said.

Amelia rushed over and joined them, staring wildly up at Black Wolf. 'What can I do?' she asked.

'I need you to stay here and treat his wounds with this paste. It'll be safer for you and I trust you to look after him,' he said, looking up at her with pain in his eyes.

'Kill us both... Birthmark... Only way,' Grey Moon mumbled to himself.

'I don't understand, Grey Moon...' Black Wolf replied, leaning in closer to try to hear his friend's words.

'It is the only way... Sacrifice.'

Black Wolf gently wafted the herbs under Grey Moon's nose and he appeared to become more alert. He reached up and grabbed Black Wolf by the shoulders, pulling him in close.

'We have a mark of our birth. It is the wound from which we left our last life. A reminder of our past from our Great Mother, one that is always travelling forward with us. It's the only way to kill the powerful ones, and that is why through all these wars, you barely got a scratch on you. If you sacrifice me, with him, the mark of the noted elder is powerful and fuses our powers into him. This is the way to defeat him; it will rid us of his presence and banish him into the world of the dead souls.' Grey Moon started to fade again once he stopped speaking.

'What about you though, Grey Moon? What will happen to you?'

'It is my time, my child. It's the only way.'

'No, I will not do it,' Black Wolf cried angrily. 'Amelia, tend to his wounds and don't leave him. I will return.'

Black Wolf marched back towards the others, his face set in stone and his eyes fixated on one thing — the dark power.

'Enough of all this trickery,' he roared at the figure. 'If you want a kingdom, you need to earn it. Take up a mortal weapon and fight me like the pitiful man you once were, not as this magic ghost.' Black Wolf picked up a sword from a dead tribesmen's hand, and threw it at the evil being's feet.

'Very well,' said the stranger, seeming slower in his movement than before the last use of his powers. 'I ask you one thing though, Black Wolf...'

'What is that?' Black Wolf asked suspiciously.

'That if we fight as men, we fight to the death.'

'I will,' Black Wolf replied, pulling his own sword loose, and walking up to face the dark power.

CHAPTER 43

Black Wolf and the evil one were stood opposite each other, enough space between them that, when drawn, their swords could just touch.

'No trickery,' Black Wolf said.

'It may have escaped your attention, Black Wolf, but because of your friend Grey Moon over there, I'm not like the rest of you,' the evil being replied, his sword hovering in the black smoke where his arm would have been. 'All I have is this ghostly prison; I cannot hold a sword with no real hand, but I can use my power to help me wield it like you do yours. This is the only trickery I shall use, you have my word.'

Nervous at the dark power's lies and trickery, and under strict orders from Lone Wolf, the men moved closer to the evil being, ready to attack and protect their leader if needed.

'Stand down, men,' Black Wolf ordered, making his men retreat again. 'I accept your claim, but no other magic,' he said to the evil one. 'I want the children moved to safety too.'

'Very well,' the evil being replied. To the children, he said, 'Go back to your families. I will deal with you all later.' The children ran into the shadows.

'It is time,' said Black Wolf, as the two opponents started circling each other, swords drawn, both waiting for the chance to deliver the first strike.

With the whole of Orgent watching, the two fighters launched into a furious battle, their swords clashing loudly, the only noise to be heard in an otherwise silent city. The dark power moved effortlessly, gliding across the floor, while Black Wolf struggled to manoeuvre around the bodies of the fallen that littered the courtyard. Black Wolf had a natural talent for fighting but the effects of the day were starting to take their toll on him and he was spending longer defending more strikes than he was creating.

***

Away from the fight, at the gates of the city, Amelia was trying to tend to Grey Moon's wounds, but found herself distracted by her fears for Black Wolf's safety.

'You need to help me move, Princess,' he said to her, trying to sit upright. 'I need to get to the steps whilst they are still fighting.'

'Black Wolf told me to keep you here though? He said it would be safest,' she replied, 'I cannot disobey him, I promised.'

'He told you to stay with me, but he didn't say where,' Grey Moon said, attempting a smile through the pain emanating from his chest. 'I am going to the steps, it is up to you whether you join me or not, but I cannot be seen.' Grey Moon managed to get to his feet with Amelia's help, and using one of the fallen tribesmen's large wooden spears to help him balance, he started to wander slowly towards the steps, staying within the shadows of the city walls.

Amelia moved on ahead and told the others of his plans whilst he walked slowly towards them.

'The evil one is distracted by the fight, so Grey Moon can walk along behind my men. That'll offer him some cover until he reaches the steps,' Lone Wolf said, signalling for his men to fan out and protect the elder.

'I can try to use my charm, if it helps?' offered Tallulah. 'Although the dark force's power might be too strong to fall for it.'

'It all helps, trust me,' said Grey Moon, catching up with Amelia and then carrying on past her, covered by the long line of tribesmen. 'Stay here, Princess, let Lone Wolf guard you,' he called back over his shoulder.

Amelia tried to defy him and followed, until Lone Wolf caught her by the arm. 'No, Princess, it's not safe.'

'I don't care, I cannot let him put himself in such great danger and do nothing about it. Black Wolf told me to stay with him,' she pleaded, trying to pull her arm free from his strong grasp.

'He also told me to make sure you stayed safe, so that is what I'll do,' Lone Wolf said, pulling her back to Tallulah. 'Please, just wait here with me, it's the only way I can protect you.'

Amelia gave in, shaking her arm free, and standing next to Tallulah. 'If anything happens, I cannot let you stop me helping,' she said, trying to control her anger.

'Trust me, Princess, if anything happens then we'll all

be there,' he reassured her, and they watched as Grey Moon continued to head slowly towards the steps of Orgent's temple.

In the centre, Black Wolf was struggling to keep up with the pace of the dark power's blows. His cuts were a lot slower and less fluid than the evil being's ghostly movements. Sensing this, the stranger put more power into his movements and lashed out violently, catching Black Wolf's sword and sending it flying from his hand as he fell backwards.

'Any last requests?' the evil being said as he loomed large over Black Wolf's fallen body, his sword pointed towards him.

'Vengeance!' cried Lone Wolf from the crowd, and he threw the sword he'd chosen from the armoury to his friend.

Black Wolf caught the handle of the sword without looking at it and held it out in front of his body, desperately trying to protect himself.

'Must we continue this?' the evil being asked, growing impatient. 'It will be this sword, then another, but it is all futile. You need to give up now, this is all hopeless.'

Overcome by a strange sense of familiarity, Black Wolf glanced at the sword in his hand, taking in the familiar shape, and his thoughts raced as a series of images flashed past in his mind. The last one he saw was as he faced evil, Esmee's injured body beside him, taking his own life to rid the palace of the evil that had come looking for him.

'Once I have taken your men, I will kill Lone Wolf and then you can have the pleasure of watching me take the girl and kill your precious princess before your very eyes,' the vile being goaded him. 'I tried before, but this time I won't fail.' He cackled loudly, glancing at Amelia and Tallulah, his eyes burning furiously.

'Use the steps!' Lone Wolf called out, distracting the evil being momentarily, as he moved round in front of Black Wolf so he could look down on all his prisoners. Still concealed in the darkness, Grey Moon had made it to the base of the steps too and crouched down amidst the other bodies, whispering quietly to himself. 'Our Great Mother, grant me one last show of strength and I promise your bidding will be done.'

With the sword in his hand, Black Wolf looked up at the dark power and saw his eyes coldly looking at the others. His body feeling stronger with the anger running through it, he screamed, 'For Aalym!' at the top of his lungs, and launched himself towards the evil one.

As his sword flew towards evil being's chest, Grey Moon used the last of his energy to throw his own body in the way of the evil one, and Black Wolf's sword passed through Grey Moon's chest and deep into the evil being. Orgent was suddenly filled with the sound of a blood-curdling scream, and a pure white flash, as the three bodies fell to the floor together. The evil being's body landed on the steps and turned to ash the minute it connected with the cold stone, the ash then disappearing without a trace, until there was nothing left.

'You've done it!' screamed Tallulah, as she ran over to him with Amelia next to her.

Dazed, Black Wolf rolled onto his side, hoping to see his opponent's dead body beside him, but instead it was Grey Moon, with the sword impaled in his chest and blood bubbling out of his mouth as he tried to speak.

CHAPTER 44

As the others made it to where Black Wolf was lying, they all stopped, shocked at seeing Grey Moon's body covered in blood. Black Wolf crawled over to him and lifted him so he was sitting up in his arms, the blood spilling all over both of them.

'No!' he cried. 'What have I done? You weren't supposed to be here, Grey Moon!'

'Hush, my child, this is the way it was meant to happen,' Grey Moon said softly, blood still running from his mouth. 'It is my time, but I need you to listen to me...'

'It's not too late, I can save you,' Black Wolf replied, desperately trying to stop the bleeding from his friend's chest.

'I will be heading to the night world soon, my child, you cannot stop this. When I'm gone, you must set my spirit free, along with all the others', as you did in your last life. We all need to move on. You can do this for us.'

'I'll do anything you need, Grey Moon. Where has the evil being gone? He disappeared.'

'He has gone to the world of the dead souls, my child. We can only hope he stays there. I will do my best to stop him coming back.' He managed to speak, whilst still coughing up blood. 'You saved us, Black Wolf; you are the true leader of men.'

'I failed you, Grey Moon — I couldn't save you. All I wanted to do was to make you proud.' Black Wolf was starting to struggle for words as he fought back the tears.

'You have always made me proud, my child. My sadness exists in the fact that you will never know just how much. I have spent my life sacrificing everything to keep our people safe, and that started with you, many years ago in the forest.' Grey Moon's eyes started to flicker shut as his body grew tired.

'What do you mean? I don't understand?'

'You... Black Wolf... my flesh and blood... my son... I love you,' Grey Moon replied weakly, and as his eyes closed for the last time, his lifeless head fell back into Black Wolf's chest.

'I love you too, Father,' was all Black Wolf could manage

before his emotions overcame him, and the tears started flooding out.

The emotion of the scene playing out before him hit Lone Wolf hard, as he remembered the faces of his own parents when he had said his final goodbyes to them. 'I'm truly sorry for your loss, Black Wolf,' he said, head bowed, before walking over to the waiting tribesmen.

Amelia held Tallulah as she cried. As much as she wanted to be at the side of her love, she knew he needed time alone to grieve. So, with a heavy heart, she walked Tallulah away, towards the emperor, who was slumped against the temple walls, his head in his hands. She helped him to his feet and took him inside.

Sat alone with his father's body, Black Wolf gently removed the sword and threw it aside, hugging Grey Moon even closer to him, as the pain of all his lives came pouring out of him amidst this cold, stony battleground.

Across the courtyard, Lone Wolf had organised the tribesmen and they were gathering the bodies of the fallen guards and natives, while the people of Orgent were collecting a huge pile of wood together in the centre.

Amelia was sat inside the temple with Tallulah and the emperor, whilst one of his helpers was tending to his cuts and making sure he wasn't badly hurt.

'I'm so sorry, Amelia; this is all my fault,' he said, still quietly weeping at the horrors he had witnessed since the evil stranger had appeared.

'You couldn't have known, Father, you were just trying to protect us,' she replied, 'We have all lost people but we've survived. Now we need to start again and make Orgent safe. The people here need their emperor to lead them again.'

'I know you're right, but I don't know if I can do this anymore,' he said mournfully. 'I've struggled since I lost your mother and all this has made me think that it is time for me to stand down.'

'You need time to rest, that's all. We still have a lot to do to get the city back again. It will take time for the wounds to heal.' Amelia smiled at her father, offering him as much support as she could muster under the circumstances.

'Thank you, Amelia. You are truly your mother's daughter,' he said. 'So brave.'

As time ticked by, the dark cloud over Orgent had

disappeared, leaving a starry night sky instead.

The bodies had been laid out by the temple steps and covered with sheets until they could perform the ceremony that was needed to send the souls safely on their way.

Black Wolf had finally left Grey Moon's side and Tallulah found him sat outside the charred remains of Orgent's gates, looking through Grey Moon's bag.

'I came to see if you were alright, Black Wolf?' she said quietly to him, not wanting to intrude if he needed space.

'I don't know how I feel, Tallulah. I'm glad we are safe but I feel so empty now that he is gone,' he said, still sifting through the strange contents of the bag.

'I really am sorry for your loss,' she said, hugging him gently from behind. 'If you want to talk, come and find me.'

'Thank you, my child, I will,' he replied, becoming aware of how much he sounded like Grey Moon at times.

Tallulah headed back into Orgent, exchanging a sad smile with Amelia as they passed each other by the entrance.

More confident in herself, Amelia sat down next to Black Wolf and put her arm round him, saying nothing.

'He had all these herbs and pastes, all magical, but he couldn't be saved,' Black Wolf said, the tears falling down his cheeks.

'He wasn't supposed to be saved, my love. He said it was his time. He did a great thing in sacrificing himself to save all of us and he knew what he was doing.' Amelia spoke gently to him, wiping the tears from his face.

'What do I do now?' he replied. 'I don't know how to live without him.'

'You live with his memory,' Amelia said, holding his face towards hers and kissing him softly on the lips. 'Our parents live on through us, Black Wolf. My mother lives in me, as Grey Moon does in you. We are the gifts they leave the world, their legacy. We cannot let it be for nothing.'

The spark between them appeared stronger than ever.

As Black Wolf continued to look through the bag, he found his book, and next to it was a wolf's tooth on a cord. Picking it up, Amelia took it from his hand and hung it round his neck. Holding the tooth against his chest with her hand, she kissed him again. 'My brave wolf heart. The true leader of men. Now is your time.'

CHAPTER 45

The dust was slowly starting to settle after the terror in Orgent. Everyone had gathered in the courtyard; the city folk were stood in a wide circle with the tribesmen, whilst the emperor was stood at the top of the stairs, with the four powers.

'People of Orgent, we have suffered a great darkness with much loss, but now it is time for us to step back out into the light again,' the emperor announced to the crowd. 'It is time for us to say goodbye to those we have lost and pay our respects to the bravery of all who fought for our survival.'

In the centre of the courtyard stood two huge funeral pyres, one for Elspeth and those from Orgent, while the other was for Grey Moon and the fallen tribesmen. The fires were raging high into the night sky and the remaining tribesmen had prepared the bodies for the ceremony.

'We are to perform an ancient rite, to both mourn the spirit and cleanse the city. For this, I call upon the leader of the lowland's tribe, Black Wolf.' The emperor stepped back and let Black Wolf take his place.

'People of Orgent, I am sorry for your loss but I offer my prayers and thanks to all of you for your courage in these times. Please feel free to mourn however you wish whilst I say a prayer from my elders, to help those who have fallen pass over in peace.' Black Wolf walked down to the pyres and signalled for the tribesmen to start putting the bodies into the fire.

'Take these souls lightly, dear Mother, and let the light of the moon grant them a chance again, with nothing but goodness in their hearts. Let them begin a new journey.' Black Wolf felt a cold chill run up his spine as he uttered the all too familiar words. Looking at Amelia, he was just grateful that this time she was safe and he wasn't saying goodbye to her.

The city's inhabitants all stood silently with their heads bowed, mourning their loss in their own personal ways, as the bodies were loaded slowly into the fire.

Over time, all the bodies were placed in the pyres, until only Elspeth's and Grey Moon's remained. Black Wolf walked over to Amelia and spoke softly to her, 'Did you want to say anything?'

Amelia smiled sadly at him and walked over to the pyre. 'I'm so sorry, Elspeth. I hope you find some peace now. I miss you, and not a day will pass when I don't think of you. Sleep well, my friend.' A tear rolled down her cheek as a tribesman slowly lifted Elspeth's body, placing it into the fire, letting the flames engulf her.

Black Wolf knelt down by Grey Moon's body, taking one last look at his face. 'Thank you for everything. I promise to try to lead our men as well as you did. I wish I had known then, what I do now. I love you, Grey Moon. My friend, my teacher, my father. Until we meet again.' He managed to hold back his tears as he spoke, and then helped Lone Wolf lift his body and place it in the fire.

Finally, with all the bodies having been given their ceremonial farewell, the space at the bottom of the temple steps was clear. Black Wolf stood there, holding Amelia, watching the flames still reaching for the beautiful, starry night sky. The emperor stepped forward again and spoke to the crowd once more.

'There is one more thing I wish to tell all of you tonight. I have served you all for many years now. In that time, I have suffered my own personal losses, just like you have. I have given it a lot of thought and would like to announce that, from tomorrow, I am standing down as ruler of Orgent. This honour will be filled by my beautiful daughter, your princess, Amelia. There will be more to announce tomorrow, but for now I bid you all goodnight. My prayers are with all those that we have lost here.'

The emperor bowed and, after a stunned silence, a ripple of applause built up around Orgent as the people showed their gratitude for his leadership. As he walked up towards the temple, Amelia caught up with him.

'Father, what are you doing? I thought you were going to take time to think before making a decision?' Amelia had been as shocked as everyone else by the announcement.

'I did, Amelia, I promise. I learnt a lot about myself whilst facing that awful power, and a lot of it I didn't like. It's your time now; Orgent needs a fresh start.' He glanced nervously at Black Wolf, over Amelia's shoulder, before kissing her on the cheek. 'Goodnight, Amelia,' he said before heading up to the temple.

Black Wolf followed the emperor into the palace, and caught up with him sitting at the table near the kitchen area. 'What is going on, Emperor? Why are you stepping down as the ruler of Orgent?' he asked.

'It's hard to explain, Black Wolf. I saw something when that thing was talking to me… Although it didn't make sense, it felt familiar,' he said anxiously. 'Then you were all talking about past lives and it made more sense, but I need your help.'

'I will help you if I can,' Black Wolf replied, confused by the emperor's nervousness.

The emperor leant across the table and put his hand on top of Black Wolf's, causing them both to have the same visions flash before their eyes. First they saw Drei Ran offering to help Majila and Esmee, before turning them away and leaving them to fend for themselves. Lastly they saw Drei Ran stood outside the palace being spoken to by an angry Kaliam, as the black smoke drifted away from the land and disappeared into thin air.

Black Wolf pulled his hand back, fighting the mixed emotion of anger and sadness that bubbled up inside him. 'It was you,' he said. '*You* were Drei Ran.'

'I didn't know,' the emperor replied, his eyes pleading tearfully. 'I'm so sorry, Black Wolf. I wish I could make amends but I can't; what has been has gone. I won't be in that position again though, and the people of Orgent deserve better than to have a coward for an emperor, so I'm handing it all over to Amelia.'

'We've all made mistakes, Emperor, you cannot blame yourself for the past. We've all moved on, we've had to. There's nothing to forgive,' Black Wolf said, realising how much they had all suffered. They needed to look forward. 'It's not fair on Amelia though — she cannot do this alone.'

'I was hoping she wouldn't be alone.'

'What do you mean?'

'It's obvious you both hold great affection for each other; I was hoping you might stay here and lead the people with her,' the emperor said hopefully. 'If we united the wealth of this kingdom with the strength and knowledge of your tribe, everyone would benefit.'

'What about Amelia's life though? She might not want

that.'

'Then that is her choice, but I'm sure she will happily accept my idea after you speak to her.'

'You need to speak to her yourself, Emperor. I cannot make decisions for her — it's not my life.'

The emperor stood. 'You only need to ask her one question, Black Wolf, and then you will both know what to do. Let your feelings for each other guide you.'

'Ask her what?' Black Wolf said, still confused.

'To marry you, Black Wolf,' he said, smiling as he patted Black Wolf on the back and walked out of the room. He'd left a ring on the table. Both men had been unaware that Tallulah was hidden nearby, listening to every word.

***

As the fires slowly dwindled, Black Wolf found Amelia sitting on the steps, quietly watching the flames. All the people had gone back into their living quarters and they were alone beneath the clear night sky. Sitting next to her, he put his arm round her and pulled her close.

'How are you, my love?' he asked.

'I feel better now. Things are slowly getting back to normal again,' she replied. 'It's still so strange, dealing with everything I've learnt on this journey, and I can't help but wonder what happens now?'

'I know,' he replied. 'But you can do what you wish; this is the start of your future.'

His words were met with silence, and as they sat closely together there was no sound other than the crackling of the fire in front of them.

'I expect you are ready to go home now?' she said, a lump building in her throat.

Black Wolf stood up and moved in front of her, gently lifting her chin with his thumb, so her eyes met his. 'My home is wherever you are. It always has been.'

'This isn't your world though, Black Wolf. I'm no fool, I know that,' she replied tearfully.

'Then I hope the princess will do me the honour of making it my world,' he said, his eyes burning with passion.

'What are you saying?' she said.

Black Wolf got down on one knee, bowing before her.

'Amelia, my love, my heart. Would you do me the honour of accepting me as yours in marriage?' he asked, feeling more nervous than ever before.

'For eternity,' was all she said, tears of joy rolling down her face, as he slipped the ring onto her finger. She looked at it in surprise. 'My mother's ring? How?'

'Your father already gave his permission,' he replied, grinning. 'He wants us to lead the people. It's a brave new dawn.'

Amelia and Black Wolf embraced each other; he lifted her off her feet and gently spun her around as the fires illuminated their love for each other. They were both lost in their own world as the passions of many lives culminated in one moment — until another person appeared from nowhere, breaking their daydream with their excited screaming.

'I knew she'd say yes!' Tallulah shouted. 'Does that mean we can all stay here like a proper family?'

Black Wolf and Amelia laughed as she nestled in, joining their hug. 'Let us see what tomorrow brings, my child,' Black Wolf said. 'I think we've made enough decisions for one night; the princess and I need our rest.'

'Why must I always have to wait?' Tallulah said sulkily to herself. 'I'll pester you again in the morning, you can be sure of it.'

'I don't doubt that,' Black Wolf replied, grinning, and together he and Amelia headed up the steps in the direction of Amelia's sleeping quarters for some much needed privacy.

'Enjoy your...rest!' Tallulah called after them, laughing cheekily to herself, then she too went off in search of somewhere to lay her head down.

With the courtyard empty, off in the gateway, a lone figure sat, quietly thinking to himself. Lone Wolf had his sack packed and he was ready to silently slip off back to the solitude he had become used to. As he sat there though, something was niggling him and he couldn't shake the troubling feeling off. He didn't know why, but som ething was stopping him from leaving.

CHAPTER 46

It had all happened so fast. Only moments earlier the air was filled with the screaming sounds of childbirth, then the sound of a crying new-born, but now there was nothing. The two ladies came out of the hut and handed the child to its father, both looking sad despite having the honour of presenting new life.

'Can I see her now?' he asked, holding the baby tightly in his arms.

'I'm so sorry, Grey Moon, there were complications. She got very sick and all we could do was save the child. She is no longer with us, I'm afraid.'

'But how did she get sick? She was fine when she came here?' he said, the pain inside him growing fast.

'We don't know, Grey Moon. She started choking at one point during the birth and was sick, but it was all black, like ash. There are ancient tales about such things and we wanted to run, but we couldn't leave the child. We are truly sorry for your loss.' The ladies bowed, and then headed back inside the hut.

Grey Moon stood in the clearing, unsure of what to do next. He had a child in his arms, his flesh and blood, his responsibility, but the child's mother was dead and he didn't know what he was supposed to do now.

'I guess it is just you and me then, my child,' he said to the baby. 'Welcome to the world.'

Grey Moon took a step forward, hoping to enter the hut and take one last look at his love, but as he did so, he noticed a strange black smoke wafting from within. The child in his arms seemed to sense something was wrong, and started crying loudly.

'Hush, my child, we must go or we will be in great danger,' he said, trying to distract the child with the wolf tooth he had hanging round his neck.

The child quietened and Grey Moon moved quickly towards the cover of the forest. No sooner had he reached it than he took a look back at the hut, only to find it had gone up in flames. The eerie black smoke seemed to snake around it, like it was hunting for something. With the child in his arms, he ran, and kept running, until he was deep in the forest near the lowlands, standing in an opening that had nothing but a broken tree stump in it.

Needing time to think, Grey Moon wrapped the child up tightly in the blankets, and placed him gently inside the hollow stump, before wandering into the forest to fetch some water. On his return he saw a large black wolf standing up against the tree stump, sniffing the inside of the stump where the child was.

'Leave him alone! Go — now!' Grey Moon shouted, throwing sticks at the large animal.

The wolf looked backwards at Grey Moon, turning in mid-air, and bared its teeth, growling angrily. Grey Moon could do nothing except sit nearby and keep watch, hoping the wolf would leave without harming the child.

Days passed like this where, eventually, the wolf allowed Grey Moon to get close enough to give food or water to his child, but whenever he tried to take him out of the tree stump, the wolf would snarl and bare his teeth again. Day and night, Grey Moon had sat nearby, watching the wolf guard his child, the tree stump littered with scratches from his claws, and eventually one day he awoke to find the wolf gone.

'I know what I must do now, my child,' Grey Moon said, quickly lifting his child out of the stump before the wolf returned, and together they headed back to his tribe.

When he reached his tribe, many natives both male and female, greeted him and asked where the child had come from.

'I had a vision from our Great Mother,' he said, 'a prophecy of a special child who could be found in the woods, so I searched for him and brought him back to us.'

'What is his name? Who is he?' a tribesman asked.

'His name is Black Wolf and one day he will be the leader of men,' Grey Moon announced, his heart breaking at having to distance himself from his child, but knowing that he had no other choice. As the child was handed over to the women to be cared for, Grey Moon swore he heard a loud cry in the distance.

'As the wolf howls,' he said to himself, sadly walking back to his hut alone.

***

In the dark tunnel, lit only by flaming torches, the silence was broken only by a single voice, 'Where are we, Grey Moon?'

'This is the night world, my friends,' Grey Moon replied. 'Take a torch from the wall; it is very dangerous in this light.'

All the men, including Grey Moon, took torches from the wall and continued their journey down the cold, damp tunnel. After they had been walking for some time, they came to a place where the tunnel split in two. One direction headed slightly uphill and the sound of running water could be heard, off in the distance, and the other direction was slightly downhill, and appeared even darker and less inviting than their current surroundings.

'What will happen to us?' asked one of the tribesmen.

'You have a choice, my friend, we all do. If you follow the higher path, this will lead you to the heart of the Lake of Essence, where you will be reborn into the world you left behind. The other path leads to the world of the dead souls. That is where I am headed.' Grey Moon spoke seriously to the men, knowing that every choice made affected the world in different ways.

'Why not come with us? Start again?' the tribesman asked.

'I still have work to do, or the living will never be safe,' Grey Moon replied. 'I will say my goodbyes now, my friends. You have the world to return to, and a long journey ahead of you.'

'We wish you well, Grey Moon. We will pray for your safe return. Until we meet again.' The tribesmen all bowed, and then headed up the higher path, towards the sound of the Lake of Essence, and a fresh start.

Grey Moon stood and watched the tribesmen walking away, until they were out of sight, then he knelt down, closed his eyes, and spoke.

'From the voice of our Great Mother, I pray that you hear me, my child. The book is yours now — you must keep it safe. All the magic of our people is held within its ancient pages, so please keep it from harm, my child. I must go now. I will keep this evil trapped here forever. Live long and well, my son. My heart is with you.' A tear ran down Grey Moon's cheek as he stood and slowly started making his way down the cold, dark tunnel, to the world of the dead souls, and his last chance of keeping his son safe for eternity.

A long way down the tunnel, in one of the dark caves that littered the walls, the evil being's ghostly body was slumped against the cold stone floor.

'I will kill you, Grey Moon, and then I will take what I need to walk from here, for good,' he said menacingly. 'Your ancient body is better than this ghostly shell.'

Then, using as much power as he could muster, a ball of flame lit up in front of him, and in it he saw the smiling faces of Amelia and Elspeth.

'I will leave here, even more powerful,' he said, 'and then your time will come.' The images vanished as the dark power's evil cackle echoed around the walls of the cave.

EPILOGUE

Black Wolf sat up in bed, drenched in sweat, with Amelia sleeping soundly by his side. The morning sun was streaming through the window and he got out of bed and dressed, as quietly as he could, so he didn't wake her. He gathered Grey Moon's sack from the floor and slipped out through the door, stopping only to look at Amelia's beautiful form, as she stirred gently in bed and then went back to a deep sleep.

Walking quietly out of the temple, Black Wolf glanced at the courtyard and noticed how different it looked after the events of the previous day. The whole space looked spotless, apart from the ashen remains of the funeral pyres, and it was so bright and quiet. He walked over to where the huge doors once stood and sat against the outside wall, with nothing but the forest and the long path leading away from the city in front of him. As he sat there enjoying the sunshine, he took his book out of the sack and opened it so he could write his latest dream in it. As the pages fell open, he noticed lots of writing and drawings inside that weren't his, and then he recalled the words he'd heard from Grey Moon in his dream: *The book is yours now, you must keep it safe. All the magic of our people is held within its ancient pages, so please keep it from harm, my child.*

'This is not my book?' Black Wolf said to himself, surprised by his discovery.

A voice came from the forest. 'You're up early, Black Wolf.' Lone Wolf appeared, looking weary.

'As are you,' replied Black Wolf. 'I had a strange night and it's left me very unsettled. It seems there is more trouble to come, if we're not careful.'

Lone Wolf sat next to his friend and listened as Black Wolf told him all about his vision of the night world, and his fear that the dark power might reappear again, and stronger than ever.

'So much that happens in this world I find no truth in, Black Wolf, but Grey Moon is a rare and powerful individual, so if he has sent you this message then it must be taken seriously.'

'I know,' replied Black Wolf, flicking through the ancient

looking pages of the book, filled with myths and magic of a bygone age. 'Grey Moon sacrificed himself to save us, but it might still not be enough. He needs my help.' The frown on Black Wolf's face showed just how concerned he was, and Lone Wolf shared his worry.

'There's nothing you can do now though, Black Wolf,' he said. 'He's already gone.'

'There is one thing. But Amelia won't like it.'

'Amelia won't like what?'

'I'll tell you once I learn more,' Black Wolf said cryptically.

'Well, I suggest you keep silent for now, my friend. It appears your lady is heading this way,' Lone Wolf said, noticing Amelia walking across the courtyard in their direction. 'I'll leave you to it,' he added, standing and wandering off inside the city walls.

'Couldn't sleep?' Amelia asked as she reached Black Wolf. 'I woke up and wondered where you were.'

'I'm sorry, Amelia, I had some visions from my birth and Grey Moon in the night world,' he replied, still visibly shaken. 'I've got his book here and I just wanted to read through it and learn more.'

'That's fine, my love, as long as you are alright...' she replied, stroking his hair. 'You've got time to yourself now. I need to prepare for this afternoon.'

'What's happening this afternoon?'

'My father wants to announce the plans for Orgent, and how we move forward,' she explained. 'So if you are going to run, you had better do it now,' she joked, bending to kiss his cheek.

'I'm not running anywhere. You are my heart, Amelia, you always will be,' Black Wolf replied, hiding the worry in his voice until Amelia turned and headed back to the temple.

Alone again, Black Wolf sat and studied the pages of the book. Everything Grey Moon knew was concealed inside its pages, including details of how to get to the night world and what awaited anyone who went there. As Black Wolf sat quietly reading, Orgent started to come alive behind him. Lone Wolf had taken charge of the tribesmen once more and half were cleaning up the remains of the funeral pyres, while the other half were helping Orgent's carpenter to build new doors for the city.

By the time Black Wolf had finished reading everything

in Grey Moon's book, it was the afternoon, and his head was spinning with all the new information he had learnt. He knew now what he had to do. He made his way back into the city, which was ready for the emperor's gathering.

Black Wolf joined the group on the steps, where they had stood together the previous evening. Amelia was wearing a red dress, another one that had belonged to her mother, and Black Wolf couldn't help but stare back at her, wishing there was another way, as the emperor addressed the crowd.

'People of Orgent, I thank you all for joining us today. It is a joy to meet you all in happier circumstances, and I hope you are all well. I have given a lot of thought to my time as your emperor and what we need as a city in order to move forward to a brighter future. I mentioned yesterday that I feel it's time I stepped down and handed rule of the city over to your princess, and I have decided that is the best course of action.' The emperor fought against his emotions as he delivered his strong speech to the people. 'So, with you all as witnesses, I call forward the princess in order to formally induct her as the new leader of Orgent.'

Amelia stepped nervously forward amongst a ripple of applause, and bowed before her father. 'Amelia, do you accept the city of Orgent and all those in it, as yours to guide, protect and rule, until such time comes that you cannot do so anymore?'

'I do, Emperor,' she replied.

'Do you take this vow, under the skies of the Great Mother, and swear to lead these people with honesty and grace?'

'I do, Emperor.'

'Then on this day, with the powers entrusted to me, I hereby hand you the throne of the kingdom of Orgent. From this day forth, the people will know you as Empress Amelia.' And as he spoke, he placed a thin, jewelled headpiece on her head. 'May your ruling age be safe and fortuitous.' Then he stepped to the back of the group, leaving Amelia in the limelight.

'People of Orgent, it is a great honour to be given the chance to lead you all, and I promise to do my best to keep you all safe and happy every day. I will strive to create a kingdom built on our new found friendship with the tribe from the lowlands, and together we will unite to provide us all with the best chance of moving into a bright new future.' Her eyes were welling up as she spoke. 'For now, I'll let you enjoy the festivities. I thank you all.'

The crowd cheered and clapped wildly as Amelia bowed and walked back to the others. As the people of Orgent started celebrating the start of happier times, there was a sombre mood amongst the group though, and they could all feel it.

'I am heading inside now; I will leave you all to enjoy yourselves,' the emperor said to the four of them. 'I'm so proud of you, my child — and your mother would have been too,' he added, hugging Amelia, before heading up the steps towards the temple.

'Thank you, Father,' she replied with a mixture of pride and sadness as she came to terms with her new role in Orgent.

Tallulah had been quiet for most of the day, but found the atmosphere starting to trouble her. Amelia felt something too, as she noticed Lone Wolf and Black Wolf had been exchanging serious glances since Black Wolf had returned from outside the walls.

'Why do I feel there is something you're not telling me?' Amelia asked. 'What's wrong, Black Wolf?'

Black Wolf tried to avoid eye contact with her. 'I need to go, Amelia. I got a message from Grey Moon last night, and today I have been reading his book, looking for guidance. The evil that has affected all our lives plans to return and finish what it started.'

'I don't understand — Grey Moon killed him. He cannot come back, surely?'

'In the book it speaks of the powerful ones and their ability to return from the night world; that is where Grey Moon and the dark power are. Grey Moon plans to destroy him and save us, but he is weaker than before and I don't think he can do it alone. I've seen the dark power and he is still strong.' Black Wolf took Amelia's hand as Tallulah looked on, the fear etched upon her face.

'What are you saying?' Amelia asked, scared of the answer she was about to receive.

'I must sacrifice myself to join him, and together we can destroy the dark power, once and for all.'

Amelia was shocked. 'You mean die? So you can join him?'

'It is all in the book, Amelia. Grey Moon died through the sign of his birth, so he couldn't ever come back into this life, but there is another way. Walk with me, all of you. I'll explain everything.' Black Wolf spoke with such calm confidence that they had to listen, and together the four of them walked through the city, in deep discussion.

Black Wolf explained everything he had learnt in the book, from the mark of birth, through to the night world and the world of the dead souls. The book had revealed the link between the faeries' Lake of Essence, and his chance to return to the world once his job was done, as long as his body was taken back to the Charmed Woods, to await the return of his soul.

As he spoke, Lone Wolf listened intently to every word, almost emotionless, whilst Tallulah sobbed constantly and Amelia argued every step of the way, until eventually they arrived outside the city walls.

'Amelia, I must do this, it is our only option,' Black Wolf said, holding her hands as they stood staring into each other's eyes. 'If there was any other way, I would do it. I don't want to leave, but if you follow the book, and all that I have told you, you can bring me back again, I promise.'

'I don't want to lose you,' she said, her voice breaking as the tears started to flow.

'You won't, my love. It has taken me a lifetime to find you again, you are my eternal heart, but I must do this.' Black Wolf felt his heart breaking, but had to try to stay strong.

'There must be another way!' Tallulah cried, throwing herself at Black Wolf and hugging him to her tightly.

'No, my child, this is the only way. You need to get my body to Ember — she will know what to do.' He kissed her head as she cried into his chest.

Lone Wolf looked at Amelia and nodded, showing her that what Black Wolf had said was true, no matter how much it hurt her to admit it.

'Tallulah, can I get one last goodbye?' Amelia asked softly, stroking Tallulah's back until she released her grip, letting her get close to Black Wolf.

'I will do whatever it takes to get you back, Black Wolf. I will not lose you,' she said, her head against his shoulder. 'I cannot believe we met too late. I must not believe it.'

'We didn't, my love; it was too soon. When I return, there is nothing in all of our Great Mother's lands combined that can keep me from you.' And they kissed, the sparks flying through their bodies as their lips met. All the passion of all their lives combined in the two lovers as they said goodbye.

Black Wolf handed his book to Amelia. 'Do everything it says and I'll return to you, my lifeblood, my Amelia,' he said, taking a small bottle out of the sack and handing her the empty bag.

Lone Wolf stood watching them; feelings were building in him as the past collided with the present once more. 'You weren't supposed to die,' he said. 'Not then, not now. I won't be left with your body again.'

'You have done so much already, Lone Wolf. I cannot ask you to come with me, but thank you, my friend.' Black Wolf embraced him and then sat against the wall of Orgent, opening the cap from the bottle and drinking the contents.

Black Wolf sat gazing at Amelia. He lifted his hand to his chest and smiled at her. 'Bring me back, my love,' was all he managed to say before his head started to droop, and his eyes closed, as if he had fallen into a deep sleep.

Amelia and Tallulah stood sobbing and holding each other whilst Lone Wolf let out a strange cry. 'You didn't ask me — I offered!' he said, revealing an identical bottle.

'You knew? How?' Amelia asked through the tears.

'Grey Moon showed me the book back at the cave,' he replied sleepily. 'I just called the men. Make sure you follow the instructions in the book, and bring him back.'

As Lone Wolf's body crumpled to the floor, the tribesmen appeared, armed with torches and ready to assist the new empress. 'We are ready for you to lead us,' one of them said, bowing before Amelia.

'We need to get back to the Charmed Woods. Tallulah, is there any way we can get back there without Grey Moon's magic?' she asked, her tears replaced by a determination to save Black Wolf.

Tallulah presented her with the pouch that Ember had given her, and spoke slowly as she tried to control her tears. 'This will reveal it to us when we get to the forest,' she said.

'Men, carry Black Wolf and Lone Wolf, and follow me,' Amelia ordered. 'We need to go now.'

As the sun set over Orgent, Amelia led the men with Tallulah at her side. Together, the group headed down the path that led to the city, determined to try to save their fallen heroes. Somewhere, a wolf howled, the sound echoing eerily around the city walls.

Author Profile

Michael Linford was born in Boscombe in 1977, and throughout his life has shown a passion for three things: music, books and people. He spent years working in music retail, which allowed him to immerse himself in music all day long. He was then drawn towards the care industry where he has spent over ten years looking after people, all of whom had stories to tell.

Having had childhood aspirations to become a writer, as an adult Michael started to pen poetry as an emotional outlet for various issues he'd suffered from throughout the years. In 2011, he wrote over 400 poems before eventually releasing two small collections of his works.

Michael combined his love for books, music and people in the writing of his debut novel entitled Music for the End of the World, which was published in December 2012. Following the novel's release, Michael became ill and, during his time recovering, returned to an earlier work that he had never completed. This fantasy novel drew inspiration from his interest in Native American and Tibetan cultures and old-fashioned tales of good versus evil. Revisiting this idea enabled him to finally complete the novel As the Wolf Howls.

For more information or to contact the author, go to:
www.facebook.com/MichaelJamesWriter

Publisher Information

Rowanvale Books provides publishing services to independent authors, writers and poets all over the globe. We deliver a personal, honest and efficient service that allows authors to see their work published, while remaining in control of the process and retaining their creativity. By making publishing services available to authors in a cost-effective and ethical way, we at Rowanvale Books hope to ensure that the local, national and international community benefits from a steady stream of good quality literature.

For more information about us, our authors or our publications, please get in touch.

www.rowanvalebooks.com
info@rowanvalebooks.com

Lightning Source UK Ltd.
Milton Keynes UK
UKOW05f1238261016
286195UK00012B/238/P